# SCOTTISH STORIES
### FROM
# MACGREGOR'S GATHERING

# SCOTTISH STORIES

## FROM

# MACGREGOR'S GATHERING

SELECTED BY

## JIMMIE MACGREGOR
## & STEPHEN MULRINE

BBC BOOKS

Published by BBC Books
a division of BBC Enterprises Limited
Woodlands, 80 Wood Lane,
London W12 0TT

First published 1989
© The Contributors 1989
ISBN 0 563 20739 6

Typeset by Phoenix Photosetting, Chatham
Printed and bound in England by
Mackays of Chatham PLC, Chatham, Kent
Cover printed by Fletchers of Norwich

# CONTENTS

# PREFACE

Since October 1982, the BBC Radio Scotland programme *Macgregor's Gathering* has been broadcast five days a week, every week.

One of the most popular regular features has been the weekly Writers' Workshop, and from the beginning it has been conducted by Stephen Mulrine. Stephen is an experienced professional, who analyses and criticises our listeners' contributions with meticulous care and a real understanding of the aspiring writer's problems. He pays people the compliment of taking their work very seriously and, in consequence, his judgments can sometimes appear to be quite severe. No one seems discouraged, for the volume and quality of submitted work steadily increase.

Quite a number of Scottish writers who are now regularly published made their first appearance in the course of my weekly talks with Stephen, and I am delighted – but not at all surprised – that *Scottish Stories from Macgregor's Gathering* maintains the high standard set by our two previous BBC publications – *Macgregor's Gathering of Scottish Dialect Poetry* and *Scottish Poetry from Macgregor's Gathering*.

Jimmie Macgregor

# TOP OF THE BILL

*Audrey Evans*

I hadn't expected a street anything like this. These houses had double garages and tennis courts in the gardens. Number 7 was mock Tudor, the walls very white, the beams very black. Standing outside the wrought-iron gates, I tried to decide what my approach to Mrs Weston should be.

A woman in an overall towing a vacuum cleaner let me in. I gave her my card and she went off, leaving me standing in the hall. I had a good look round. Dark polished floor, a long-case clock, a Chinese rug, creamy roses in a crystal bowl, copies of *Country Life*. I picked one up, and had just decided on an Old Rectory with stabling and paddock, when a voice behind me spoke.

'Mr MacLean?' Mrs Weston, and at first glance, a very pleasant sight; smoky grey hair, clear blue eyes and a trim figure. Silk, cashmere and pearls, voice crisp as a biscuit. She was looking at my card. 'You have – television connections?'

'I'm sorry. That was the only card I had with me. I apologise for calling on you without an appointment, but I have to be in London this evening. After that it would be difficult for me. If you could give me a few minutes of your time, I would be grateful.'

Mrs Weston thought it over and decided in favour of my expensive suit. 'Very well,' she said, and led me into a sitting room that was a natural extension of the hall, all chintz, framed prints, and more roses. Mrs Weston waved me to an armchair and sat, poised and attentive, on a sofa.

I had decided what I should say. 'Mrs Weston, I'm a writer. At present I am engaged in research for a book on the Variety Theatre, stars of the Variety stage. I . . . I hoped you could help me.'

She glanced at my card, still in her hand. 'I'm afraid there must be some mistake. There is no way in which I could be of help to you. I have no knowledge of, or interest in, that kind of theatre.'

I should have gone then, apologising for troubling her. But I tried again. 'It's the later variety theatre. The 1930s and after. The Scottish theatre as well.'

'It sounds very interesting,' she said, and leaned forward to give me back my card, 'but I can't think why you have come here.'

I was being patronised, and it made me angry. 'You *are* Roddy Stark's daughter, aren't you?'

Mrs Weston's face had fine bones under a delicate cosmetic mask. It fell easily into planes of disdain. 'Who sent you here? Are you some kind of journalist?'

'I wasn't sent by anybody.' I took a breath. 'Although I've talked to people.'

'People? What kind of people?'

'An old theatre dresser called Bernard Gibson.'

And to my surprise and relief, she gave a whisper of a laugh and said, 'Bernie? Is he still alive? He must be about a hundred. What did he have to say?'

'He told me about working – about working for your father. And he said that Roddy Stark was the greatest comedian he had ever known. Not just a Scots comedian, *the* greatest. Mrs Weston, you must be able to remember him. It would be of great help to me.'

'He died when I was a baby.'

'You were twelve when he died.'

Her eyebrows went up. 'Extensive research,' she said, and waited in composed silence for me to give up. I tried again.

'I'm sorry. I haven't been quite frank with you. Although I would like very much to write the kind of book I described, the reason I'm so interested in Roddy Stark – this is going to take some time, I'm afraid.'

She looked at her watch. 'You may have ten minutes, Mr MacLean, and you should be prepared to be disappointed at the end of them.'

'Well. I do have a connection with television. I was responsible for the BBC show, *Gold and Silver*. It ran for four series. You may have seen me in it.'

'I don't possess a television set,' she said.

That set me back. I suppose that if I had had a picture of Roddy Stark's daughter, it was of a little woman in a bungalow some-where, being bowled over by the appearance of the well-known television personality. Faced with Mrs Weston, now looking thoughtfully at her fingernails, I ploughed on. 'It was a bit like old-time music hall. We recreated the great theatre personalities of the past. People like Jack Buchanan and Jessie Matthews.'

Her face was so expressionless that I thought she was going to say that she had never heard of them.

'Anyway, after the last series ended, we took it on the road. We've been touring for three months now, and it's a smash hit.' I thought she looked faintly incredulous, and found myself explaining. 'Nostalgia perhaps, a craze, we get a lot of young people in . . . Anyway, we open in the Royal Theatre in Southampton on Monday, and it's booked solid. After that it's Brighton, and then London and the Victoria Palace. This is my only free day in Southampton, and I came to see you. Mrs Weston, you must have seen your father's act. You must remember.'

'Oh, I do,' she said, serene. 'And I never liked it. It was crass and vulgar.'

I was silencèd.

'Time is passing, Mr MacLean.'

Well, here goes, I thought. 'Mrs Weston, Roddy Stark's act is in the show. It's the star turn. And I play Roddy Stark.'

For the first time, she showed a kind of feeling. Her face flushed faintly and her mouth tightened. 'Do you mean that you impersonate my father? You don't look in the least like him. Although you do have the accent.' She made it sound like a skin complaint. 'How on earth do you make yourself understood in Hampshire?'

'Like Billy Connolly,' I said. I was getting angry again. 'I've got two spots in the programme. In the first half I do "The Referee." In the second, I've put together an act made up of his best routines.' I remembered the last night of the Manchester run. 'Dammit, Mrs Weston,' I said, 'I'm good.'

She went back to sounding contemptuous. 'And you feel that any childhood reminiscences I can summon up will make your – your "act" – even better?'

'I've done everything,' I said. 'I've got it right in so many ways: the walk, the hands . . . I got hold of some scripts, there were a few film clips, radio – I tracked down everybody who could tell me how he worked. They all say it's a first-class impersonation. But somehow, I've never got to the heart of him. And I hoped you could tell me about him.' I waited, but Mrs Weston was silent. When I spoke, I could hear my voice cracking in disappointment. 'And all you could say was that he was crude and vulgar.'

Mrs Weston rose and walked quickly to the window. I waited for my dismissal, but she said, looking out, fiddling with the edge of the window curtain, 'Mr MacLean, I haven't been frank with you, I admit. On the other hand, you have been lying to me. In spite of that I think you must be an honest man, with an honest reason for wanting . . . wanting to know . . . There is very little to tell, you understand. My parents were divorced when I was ten. My mother remarried; a wealthy man. I was very fond of my step-father, incidentally. I am a widow now, as I suppose you know. My son is an accountant here in Hampshire, my daughter married a diplomat and lives in Vienna.' She turned from the window. 'My point in telling you all this is that for all that time I have lived a life that was, oh, on another planet from the kind of existence I knew as a child.'

'I wish you could tell me,' I said. I was nearly on my knees, begging her. 'Please tell me.'

And she did. She sat in silence a long thirty seconds, shrugged and hesitated, but she told me. 'My mother met my father when she was on holiday in Scotland. She was a schoolteacher from Cambridge, quite young. They married almost at once. And then she . . . and later, with me, a small child . . .' Mrs Weston looked back, dismayed, at herself and her mother. 'What kind of life do you think it was for us! The horrible theatre digs, the endless, dreary train journeys on Sundays, the sweaty, beery dressing rooms, the times when there was no money at all . . . He did summer shows in places like Largs and Ayr; that wasn't so bad, but mostly I remember being cold and frightened in Glasgow. I hated it, and I suppose I was frightened because my mother was. One night in the street, a drunk came staggering up to us. He just swooped on me, picked me up and wouldn't let me go.' Mrs Weston shuddered, sitting there in her expensive clothes and jewellery. 'My God, the stink of him . . . My mother started to scream, the drunk got ugly, the police came. That night, I could hear her and my father quarrelling again. The worst night I've ever known.' She stopped, looking inward.

'But – there must have been good times surely,' I said. 'He was top of the bill for years.'

'What? Oh, yes, I suppose so. But that meant the drunken noisy parties, the flashy hangers-on. And there was the terrible strain that nobody except my mother saw, the anxiety of being at the top. It had to be the theatre with him. Radio was no good – you had to see him. Films? They were a shadow of what he was like. He had to be on a stage, at peak performance every night. Mother had to live with that.'

'Can you tell me what he was like offstage? In private?'

There was a long pause. 'Well . . . affectionate, I suppose. He used to take me to the pictures a lot till Mother put a stop to it – they were terrible little flea pits. He was crazy about Laurel and Hardy. ''Watch the timing, my wee lamb,'' he used to say.' A faint smile, then Mrs Weston tugged at her pearls, smoothed her fashionable skirt and said briskly, 'After the divorce, my mother moved to Hampshire. I only saw him once after that. I did say there was little I could tell you. And your time is up.'

As she showed me out, she said, 'I hope your – your performance goes well.'

Halfway down the path, I remembered the two front row tickets for the Monday show, intended for the little woman in the bungalow, who would have been so grateful. I went back and shoved them through the letter box.

On Monday night, I sat in my dressing room, stroking on the old-fashioned greasepaint. As usual, I was depressed at the thought of going on, and not getting Roddy Stark right.

I can't really describe his act. He didn't dress up or use props. He just stood there in a shabby suit, a scarf and a bunnet. And, well, he soliloquised. He talked about things that the audience knew; the stairheid, the steamie, the fitba', the whippet, the Palais, the disastrous trip doon the watter. And of course, 'ma faimily': his son-in-law, his wee lad and his teacher, his mother-in-law, and of course, his wife, who with her malice and eccentric cunning, thwarted his every desire.

Like all the great Scots comedians, he had a simple tag, a catch phrase. When he spoke of his wife: 'Her!' he would say, downtrodden and awed, 'Her, she's an awfy wee wumman!' Eagerly awaited, and for its precise, needle-point timing, received with a great roar of delight.

As I looked into the mirror at Roddy Stark's greasepaint mask imposed on my own face, I wondered for the first time what he had felt before he went on. He had plenty to consider. The wife who hated the life that his genius bought – and by God, they must have been well off; he commanded top salary for years. The little daughter taught to despise her father's art. The divorce that took his daughter from him, and the miles set between them that kept her away.

Poor sod, I thought. And that was it. My painted face in the glass, Roddy Stark's face, reflected something new, something that had been missing all along from my creation of the man. Pain, and fear of further hurt. 'Her, she's an awfy wee wumman!'

So she was, the bitch.

That night, onstage, I brought Roddy Stark back from the dead. I stood inside his skin, and his loneliness and rejection edged the gags, the business, the jokes. The audience were mine, to be ravished at will into hysterical abandon. At the end, coming back for the fourth curtain, I saw through the sweat that the two seats in the front row were empty.

On the way to my dressing room, the stage doorman gave me a note. It was neatly written, and it said: 'Dear Mr MacLean, You were very good. I enjoyed the performance. Thank you for the tickets. Sincerely, Margaret Weston.'

Well, that's something, I thought, looking at the stiff little message.

'Fan of yours?' said the doorman.

'What? Oh . . . yes.'

'I thought so,' he said, grinning. 'Pity she didn't know you were supposed to be funny. Crying her eyes out, she was.'


# A TURN FOR THE BETTER

*Iain Campbell*


'Best behaviour is the main thing.' The Master stopped and scanned the class. 'If, by some remote chance you forget your party piece . . . which you won't, will you? . . . then recite the first verse of the 23rd Psalm.'

He nodded towards the sound of snapping fingers, Mary McEwan's, desks up from where Calum and I sat.

'Please Sir, I've known mine for months.'

'Listen to the bitch,' Calum whispered.

'Good, Mary. But I wasn't really referring to you, dependability being your second name, almost.'

Calum jumped to his feet. 'Please Sir, I don't know mine. I only remembered about it this morning. It's a poem about ducks you gave me.'

'Ducks? I can't remember giving anything like that out.'

'Well you did, Sir. I kind of thought at the time it was an odd thing to learn.'

'Just make sure you do.'

'I might have to change a few words though, it's pretty dead for a concert.'

'You'll change nothing! Not one word of . . . of . . . whatever it is, will be tampered with. And that goes for the rest of you!'

'That's got him going,' Calum whispered as he slipped back on to his seat.

'Will there be many folk there, Sir?' wee Tam asked as if it would make any difference. He'd wander across the stage, oblivious to what was happening, if past concerts were anything to go by.

'Packed! Three hundred good-living, God-fearing people. And all educated enough to know when someone's forgotten or changed their words, Tam.'

'My mother's going, Sir, and she doesn't fear God . . . or anybody else. And I'm pretty sure she doesn't know any poems about ducks. She knows one about a wee cock sparra, though. D'ye want to hear it?'

'Don't bother, Tam.' He cleared his throat nervously. 'I know it.'

'Is there a barra in yours, Sir?'

He ignored the question, and cleared his throat again. 'What piece have you, Tam?'

'None Sir. I used to till my mother found out I eated them before I reached the school. But I can last out till dinner time fine now, Sir. My mother says I'm fair full of will-power. We've all got some . . . one of those droll things, it's there but you never see it. At least, I've never seen mine yet . . .'

'The concert, Tam, what did I give you to learn?' His words were slow and precise. 'Wasn't it "The Village Blacksmith"?'

'No Sir, I think it was about a tree of some kind. It doesn't matter anyway because I'm going to do something about ducks. We've got three. Do you know you've got to boil a duck's egg for a terrible long time, for the poison? . . . I might tell them that.'

The Master had, as usual, cut communications.

Tam turned to face our desk. 'Don't worry, Calum, I'll help you if you get stuck.'

We had no practice runs. The Master believed 'trust' was a major thing in life and the concert would be our first step in public to prove ourselves. I practised my piece each night in bed, till I was sure the beetle it concerned was tapping to me from the room wall.

Concert night seemed to skip time. The nerves I thought would go when I knew my part, simply slipped over to boost the others which pecked around 'standing in front of three hundred God-fearers.'

Calum had kept his progress with the duck thing private, over the weeks, right up to the last day. 'It's called speed reading,' he said. 'I read about it months ago. So far all I know about the ducks is the page number. Just before I'm due to go on, I give the page a very deep look and think hard, harder than ever I did in my life. It says the words get burned into the brain and that's you with a photograph memory.'

The hall was packed as promised. From the front row I listened or rather, watched, the Minister then the Master talk to the audience. Panic had blocked all sound when I couldn't remember even the name of my poem. And I noticed Calum had lost his smug look.

It felt as if a ton weight was lifted from my head when I sat, after what I thought a good performance of the 23rd Psalm.

The Master had trouble finding words good enough in praise of Mary McEwan. She glided on to thunderous applause, clasped her hands and closed her eyes and waited for silence. Tam left her on her own and the clapping died.

The main bout of the evening . . .

'The Lily Of The Valley, recited by Mary McEwan.' She paused . . . 'The Lily Of The Valley . . .' She sniffed. Then, to the hushed expectant audience she burst into a wonderful perform-ance of sobbing. She was like a fly in Tam's web.

He scuttled out and put his arm round her. 'Are you stuck, Mary?' He peered into the glistening face. 'I would do the 23rd Psalm for you if I knew it.' He led her off, again to thunderous applause.

The Master appeared wearing a smile as forced as sweet rhubarb. 'Ladies and Gentlemen, I'm sorry to say Mary isn't feeling very well . . .'

'She's fine, Sir, she just forgot the words.' Tam was at his side.

'It's a damned hard thing to learn if *she* got stuck. Are you going to say it for her?'

'Ladies and Gentlemen, Calum McKay!' Still wearing his skeleton grin he dragged rather than led Tam off the stage.

Hands deep in his pockets, Calum studied something on the ceiling for a time, then began: 'The Drake's Drum, told by Calum McKay. Oh the drake is on its hummock . . .' he roared . . . then stopped to think. 'Oh the drake is on the burning hummock . . . his feathers they are lit . . .' And as we waited to hear what word he'd use to rhyme, Tam crossed the stage, shaking his head.

'You're wrong, Calum. Never mind the 23rd Psalm; I'll do the poem for you.'

Calum slinked off, leaving Tam on his own. He waited for the coughs and feet-shuffling to die. 'Calum's poem, by me. Drake is in his hammock and a thousand miles away . . .' He walked to the front of the stage and looked down. 'Captain art thou sleeping there below?' He pretended to listen for a moment, then shook his head and told the hall: 'He's lying 'tween the round shot in Nombre Dios bay, and dreaming all the time of Plymouth Hoe . . .'

With dramatic gestures to suit the words, he went through the poem. '. . . He'll drum them up the Channel as he drummed them long ago.' He ended by saluting the completely silent and amazed audience. 'That was Calum's. Now for mine. Do youse know you've got to boil a duck egg . . .' An explosion of sound stopped him in amazement. For a moment he thought he was the cause of emptying the hall, when three hundred people got to their feet.

'I'm sorry,' he stuttered with fright. 'I thought you'd want to know about my duck eggs.'

The shouts of ''Core, More, More' finally got through and he realised they were cheering. They were cheering him! He was being thanked . . . for something. He raised his arms, like Moses, and it worked. Immediate silence.

'You gave me a fright, there. I thought you didn't want to hear my bit. It's for the poison, you've got to boil them a terrible long time. How it gets into them in the first place, God only knows.' He saluted smartly and walked off the stage.

The Master showed he was cross by not giving Mary her usual 'good morning' as we filed into the room. We sat, waiting for the climax of his angry stare. He walked slowly to the front row. 'Never, in all my teaching career, have I had the honour of being in such a religious company.'

Calum hated sarcasm.

'Out of thirty, twenty-four opted for the Psalm.' He stopped at my side. 'One of you even managed to get the verses mixed.' Calum sprung with me at the sound of a slap on the back of my head. 'One of you decided to do something really different . . .' Sarcasm coated every word. 'Didn't they, Calum? Something about a drake bursting into flames?'

Calum jumped to his feet, white with rage. 'At least I tried. Not like your wee pet at the back, she made a right balls-up.'

'Calum McKay! . . . Get out to the fr . . .'

'Calum McKay, my arse! Wee Tam did my bit!'

'Get out to the . . .'

'I'll not get out anywhere! You never praised Tam for saving your fu . . . f . . . fu . . . your concert. If it was her, we'd never hear the end of it . . . You're too bliddy busy looking for faults in other folk . . . You can expel me or do whatever the f . . . hell you want, I'm going!'

He did, with a slam of the room door.

I forced myself not to break the silence that followed. Like most of the class I agreed with Calum.

White-faced, the Master walked slowly to the front. 'I was coming to you, Tam. You gave a wonderful performance.'

'It just shows you how keen folk are to know about duck eggs, but it was Calum's idea.'

'I meant the poem, Tam,' he said as he sat on the edge of the desk-lid. 'I believe you are the first person in the old hall's history to get a standing ovation.'

'I got the fright of my life when they ovationed, Sir.'

'Who taught you it, Tam?'

'Me, Sir. Some nights I've got a job sleeping, so I have a look through books my father left me. But I only learn things I like. I know some great ones about digging for gold and wolves and things.'

'Well Tam, it's thanks to you that . . .'

'Calum has thanked me already, Sir. He's taking me to see the Millars' TV tonight. . . . I know a good one called "Dangerous Dan Magrew"; d'you want to hear it? In place of these alphabet sums?'

'I do, Tam, not right now but I do.'

'I might have to leave the camp sooner than I thought, if he expels me,' Calum said as we waited for Tam at the Millars' gate.

'I think you expelled yourself, so it's not so bad.' But I knew he was worried.

Tam arrived on his bike and dressed in his Sunday clothes. We were half-way to the door when it opened and the Head Master appeared.

'Good evening, boys,' he said as he passed.

Tam and I mumbled a reply. A few steps later he stopped. 'Calum? I'd like a word, please.'

He turned, and scuffing the pebbles with every step, went back. 'What?'

'Are you still interested in prehistoric animals?'

'The same as I was before.' He stared at the ground.

'I've a book on the subject I'd forgotten all about. Would you like to see it?'

'I'm not fussy, Sir . . . but if it's there I might as well.'

'You can pick it up at school tomorrow.'

'I'll do that, Sir.'

'Now go and enjoy your television. What's on, by the way?'

'I haven't the faintest idea, Sir. But I promised Tam and I don't like breaking my word.'

'Would you like to apologise for this morning's actions?'

'No Sir. I meant every word I said . . . but it's past now . . . isn't it, Sir?'

'It's past,' he said quietly, and turned towards the gate, a flicker of a smile in his eyes. He expected that answer. And deep down he'd hoped for it.

# JACK AND LEE DROP IN FOR A SMOKE

*Angus Watson*

She couldn't be sure, not keeping clocks or watches in the house, but when the dog barked it seemed early for the Postman Routine to be getting under way.

Every day John the Post drives down the hill in low gear, racing the engine, then revs loudly twice in the hope that she will come to the gate. She never does. Sheba starts to bark as the Postie struggles with the loop of fence wire that holds the gate shut, and the rage of dog and man grows until the letter box opens and John tries to thrust the mail past the black curled lips and the dripping teeth without injury to his hand. All that fury! Just for a news-paper, and now and again some junk mail or a bill. Then they both retreat, he to the gate, Sheba to her box, muttering under their breath. Six times a week for nine years this has gone on; and neither of them seems to tire of it and neither of them tries to intro-duce the tiniest variation.

But this time the barking went on and on and there was no slap of paper hitting the porch floor. When she got to the door a stranger was just turning away beyond the gate, shaking his head at someone in the blue pickup she could make out through the trees.

'Hullo. Can I help you?' She could have let him go, but in this quiet part of the island she didn't see many people since her hus-band had left. And she felt in the mood for company today.

'So there ye are,' he called, turning to fiddle again with the gate he had just fastened. He was tall and lean. Narrow eyes and a big jaw and that kind of steely blue-grey hair that tells nothing of age, since you can see it on a man of thirty as often as on one of fifty or sixty. It was when his mouth formed a wry smile and the lines deepened about his eyes that she recognised him.

Lee Marvin! In her garden!

'We're lookin fer auld furniture. Sideboards, chests o drawers an that. Gie ye a guid price. Cash on the nail.'

She had watched all his films on TV. He frightened her of course. Amoral. But attractive. Like a mountain lion. She didn't want him to walk out of her life again, just like that.

Something about furniture he'd said. And she thought of the mahogany wardrobe, so massive that her grandfather when he built the house had to hoist it to the upper floor with block and tackle and manhandle it to where it still stood. Then the narrow stair he'd made to let his descendants up and down had imprisoned it, seemingly for ever.

'Naw, it might tak tae bits, ye ken. We've a workshop doon in Stirlin. A' the tools like.'

As she let him in he sidled round Sheba, weighing her up. 'Dis he bite?'

'She's been known to.'

'Aye weel, that's whit ye keep 'em fer.'

Impressed by the wardrobe, Lee Marvin spent some time searching inside for places where it might dismantle. 'Ye dinnae mind if A get ma brither in tae hae a look? We'll be back this way next week, an if he likes it we could aye strip it doon an tak it aff yer hauns then.'

He came back in, bringing the other man, and she stood at the door again to shepherd them past the dog. She could see the resemblance without a doubt. Though the second man's hair was black he had the same long frame, the same elongated skull – though thinner, with high cheekbones – and the same narrow eyes.

Jack Palance! She didn't know they were brothers. But then movie stars don't use their real names, do they?

'I recognised you at once,' she said as the men moved lithely up the stairs, two and three at a time. 'Och we're decent enough guys,' said Lee, 'tryin tae mak an honest penny.'

They knew their script well, chatting easily about presses and aumries, veneers, Victorian chests, barley twists. Jack Palance dismissed her best dressing table as 'Jist Repro.'

Then Lee lit a cigarette.

Now nobody, but nobody, smokes in her house, violating the air she breathes. But then you don't tell Lee Marvin what he can and can't do. On a screen in her head there played in slow motion the scene where he throws a man through a window to splatter on the sidewalk far below. Then she saw the Saint Andrew's cross made by her own body's exit through the pane, with Lee dusting his hands as he watched her hit the flowerbed, her gingham skirt up about her thighs.

He replaced the lighter in the pocket of his windcheater and she glimpsed the gunmetal sheen of his Magnum.

Jack Palance was smoking too now, the cigarette aimed at her navel, the smoke drifting lazily upwards. As he talked, she watched the lengths of ash forming, waiting in vain for him to shake them into the waste bin. 'Ye dinnae still hae the top fer the 'drobe, Hen? Wi the top we could hae got a hunnerd an fufty fer it, nae bother, efter we'd got it back tae Dundee an din it up. We'd hae gien ye a hunnerd on the spot an made fufty fer oorsels.' He patted the hip pocket of his jeans, bulging with a wad of greenback dollars. 'As it is, we cannae gie ye mair na therty.'

When she didn't react, 'Straight up,' he said, taking a step forward. 'I hope ye dinnae think we're tryin tae rip ye aff.'

She knew this was the hard-bitten renegade of *I Died a Thousand Times*, but she knew too that he had a heart. Didn't he love Shelley Winters so much that it brought him to his death? Poor Shelley! Such a pity she went to fat. While here was Jack Palance standing in her bedroom, still as lean as a stoat.

As he raised the cigarette to his lips and hooded his eyes even more against the smoke, his half-rolled shirtsleeve slid further up, baring tattooed serpents embracing a Death's head.

Lee seized him by the arm. 'That maks me bloody livid, that dis.' He was pointing to the split in the wardrobe drawer that her brother had made years ago when he had had to burst the lock. Together the men bent and opened the drawer, then stood side by side, staring down. They had exposed a jumble of bras and pants. Blues and pinks and whites. And a suspender belt she hadn't worn since the days of her marriage and had never bothered to throw away.

As Lee turned towards her, opening his mouth to speak, there was the sound of a vehicle scurrying down the hill and revving noisily at the gate. 'It's yer lucky day, Hen,' said Jack Palance, looking past her out of the window. 'Here's Postman Pat.'

Sucking in her stomach, willing her breasts to contract, she squeezed between the men and the double bed she had never changed for a smaller one, and went down the stair. John the Post looked at the two men who followed her out of the house but he didn't speak. As they watched him go she put her foot on Sheba and pushed her to the ground, holding her there. 'Ye bide alane, dae ye?' asked Lee. She released the pressure of her foot just a little and looked him boldly in the eye. 'I have the dog.'

'Onywise,' Jack Palance broke in, 'we'll phone roond the dealers, see if we can get a top tae fit, 'n if we dae we'll gie ye yer hunnerd when we're back up, in a couple o months.'

'Gie's yer phone number,' Lee Marvin drawled as they left. 'Tae phone about the 'drobe, like.' She didn't refuse. I mean, Lee Marvin asking for your phone number!

She watched their pickup drive off into the bright sunlight, then went back indoors.

The spent slugs of their cigarette ash she swept up straight away, the smell of smoke lingered in the air for a day or two, but Jack and Lee didn't phone and they didn't come back. Not in a week, and not in a couple of months. She thought the Sheriff had probably caught up with them in the end.

# PRIVATE McNAB'S PRIVATE BATTLE
## Lydia Duncan

He taen the sneck aff the windae, an stickin his tongue in an O shape atween his lips, blew ae smoke ring then anither. Up they floatit, twa near perfeck circles till they met wi the in-comin wun. They bobbit for a meenit then wur poud oot o shape an souked awa like Wull o the Wisps. Gin he wur Pegasus, he thocht, wi weengs on his baffies, he'd flee efter them.

He settled doun on the wuiden lid o the lavvie sait, lichtit anither fag an cairried oot a mental recce. It didnae metter hou he luiked at it, he cud see nae wey oot – no this time, onywey.

The chappin at the door broke his dwammin. 'Are you in there, William?'

He pit his thoum tae his nose an stuck oot his tongue aince mair in a silent gesture o protest. She kent damn fine he wis, but Wullie nivver lat dab. He gae a lang drag on the doupie. 'Bath time. Coo-eee . . . William, are you listening?'

Fine he heard an fine he felt that same auld feelin. She'd gien him a bath aince afore an that wis aince ower often – a lassie nae muckle mair than a bairn. She'd bathed him an damned near drouned him in a sea o shame.

'Mr McNab?'

In the meenit's saucht, he cud hear the duntin o his ain hert.

*'O, whit a panic's in thy breistie!'*

'Come along, William. . . . There's a good boy.'

Good boy – Pretty boy! He cocked his heid tae ae side. Ye'd hae' thocht he wis a bluidy budgie cornered in a cage. There wis a steir in the lobby an the young auxiliary lat him be. He kent the skreichin vyces. Argie bargie, aa day lang.

*'Wi' bickering brattle!'*

There wis a constant fecht aboot fouterie things atween Miss Whyte an Nell Nicoll. Gin they cud, they'd hae a joustin match wi their zimmers. He wearied o their fechtin. He'd seen real fechtin in his day – up tae the oxters in glaur – the plets o his kilt hotchin wi lice.

'Send in the Jocks,' said the 'High Heid Yins.' They gaed in, but no mony o them cam oot. An whan the fechtin wis ower, they'd preened a medal on his kist.

'Well done, Jock – old chep.' A haunshak, a pat on the back an intae yer civvies.

He'd fund himsel in tichter spots afore the day. Then there wis Swankie the warden tae contend wi. Wullie couldna thole the wee man.

*'Wee sleekit, cowrin', tim'rous beastie!'*

Carin staff they'd tellt him tae. The Social workers hud even likened the home tae a fower-star hotel. Wullie hud considered suin them for a contravention o the Trades Descriptions Act. He thocht on the place mair on the lines o a five-star nut hoose; an tae add insult tae injury, aa the inmates wur weemin bar himsel.

Somebody hoasted ootside, tried the haunle, then he heard the familiar wheenge. 'Wid ye hurry up in there?'

He souked on the fag then flaffed his airms aboot tae disperse the reik.

Big Bella spoke again, soundin mair agitated. 'Am burstin.'

The lavvie in the ootside lobby wis his ae refuge an he wisnae budgin. Abune the smell o reik an disinfectant, the waff o pee an decay hung in the air. The wun steired the tossles on the curtains. His fingers wur gaein deid an he cud feel the cauld seipin throu his baffies fae the tiled flair. He rubbed his hauns thegither then stuid up tae sneck the windae. His ain reflection gowked back at him fae the coloured gless – a wizened auld face – no the face o a fechtin sojer lad ava.

> 'But, och! I backwards cast my e'e
> On prospects drear!
> An forward, tho' I canna see,
> I guess an fear.'

He stertit – Swankie wis rattlin at the door – the camp commandant himsel! But whit wis that he wis shoutin? 'Rauchen verboten. . . . Raus raus!'

Wullie heard the rattle o keys, made tae nip oot his fag then dachled. He eyed the wyste paper basket plettit wi rashes. 'Bombs away.' He flicked the fag end an watched it smouder. His aim wis true, richt on target. He felt in his pouch for the wee book o Rabbie's rhymes, poud the weel worn pages an lat them faa. Wee fluffs o smoke curled canny like up ower the green, crackled tiles then the reid gliff kinnled intae life. Aa Hell wis lat lowse. There wis a great steir ootside the door.

He held oot his hauns tae the heat then hunkered doun tae enjoy the last fag in the packet.


# WEB

## Kate Armstrong


Maggie crouched on the step below where the bee attempted to cant itself forward into the grass. Without wing-power this seemed impossible. Had she really never seen a bee walk before? All those legs ought to be good for something. The wings were so firmly overlapped along the furry back that they seemed welded together, and could surely never have lifted the bulky, barrel-shaped body. It was odd to be so near a bumble bee, odder still not to feel the wings' fanning, oddest of all not to hear the adrenalin-boosting buzz. What made the buzz anyway – legs? antennae? a voice in a corner of her mind demanded.

There's a great deal you don't know, announced another, but that question's not relevant. Your thinking is in a tangle.

What matters, said a third, a rather Maggie-like voice, is that this bee is unable to be a bee. It has just attempted to clean its legs, but given up, probably exhausted, and we don't know if bees can use their legs to clean their wings anyway. You can't touch its wings, even were your paintbrush soft squirrel and not scratchy hogshair; you'd damage them.

Stepping carefully over the creature, she brought in the garden chairs and the dry washing. Really, the garden was a mess. The compost bin was overflowing, needed emptied. The wind had toppled and scattered a stack of dirty plastic flower pots. Huddles of dead leaves reminded her that the splintery-handled rake had not been used for a long time. The sun was low, and barely warm enough for her to work outside. Certainly it was not warm enough to dry out a bumble bee's wings, assuming they were simply still undeveloped, unready for use because they had only known life in a cool, damp, sunless shed.

Surprised at how much help her mind was proving, now she had stopped trying to focus on bees, she thought what a lot of things had to go just right for a creature to be itself – unless, of course, one included in that achievement becoming a spider's dinner, or a desiccated corpse in a grubby corner.

The problem bubbled gently away, like a reliable coffee-pot, as she washed dishes, scraping and wiping, rinsing and stacking. As she dried her hands, the helpers moved forward.

Bees are fed through the winter on sugar syrup, said the brisk, pedagogical voice from behind her right eyebrow. Honey in the summer months, though in poor summers they need sugar syrup to top up their honey reserves.

Bees are bees, declared another, neutral but friendly. All bees need honey or nectar or pollen.

The voice that asked, White or brown? was brushed aside as she poured water from the kettle onto a spoonful of golden granulated in a saucer. To the query, Too warm? she did not reply, but stepped briskly through the fast-cooling garden, pot and silver spoon in hand, to where the sun's rays just reached the top step and the motionless bee.

Very gently, she depressed the grass-blades with the back of the loaded spoon, just in front of the angular, inefficient legs that tapered to narrow, wispy hairs. Would he smell the syrup? Apparently not. Not in one second, not in ten. Very gently, she let a drop spill onto the thread-like foot. It is reasonable to wait, be patient, she told herself. A tiny movement trembled down the leg's length, and the foot lifted a fraction, slowly, wavered and gradually returned to its previous position. No, not quite. He was bending it, and the other front leg too.

The proboscis was almost half an inch long. It found the nearest part of the spoon's bowl with accuracy and ease, it seemed. The minute, bright-brown tongue that emerged was forked at the tip, and seemed only to operate at right angles to its casing. At most, she thought, an eighth of an inch, but sweeping in and out so fast that it was hard for her to gauge the size, and flexing invariably back towards the body, drinking where the syrup was shallowest. Cold and stiff, she knew she would hold that spoon just right, for as long as was needed.

He stopped. How much? Perhaps a raindrop's worth. She ran a mental inventory of his state as it seemed to her.

Two days ago she had seen him trapped when she was in the shed for firewood, and had thought, it must be spring if the bumble bees are around again. Not that we see many – perhaps just one in a garden this size. The following day, when she had gone out to put groceries in the freezer, he had still been there, two legs firmly tangled in an ancient, draught-draggled spider's web, and she had thought him dead, probably of cold, a fixture where the frame met the grimy frosted glass, beyond the lawnmower and the garden canes. Today, snatching out a pint of milk to replace one she had spilt, she had heard the faintest buzz, seen him wrench and yank at the clinging, sticky grey anchors, and, practical person that she was, had scooped him carefully into a flowerpot, web and all, and carried him to where the evening sun cast long grass-blades over the top step.

She had run for a paint brush. It had served only to pull on and straighten the fragile legs, and the joined wings flapped frantically for a moment, rearing him half-up, only to topple half-down, neither flying nor grounded. The bottle-brush was better, its nylon bristles catching firmly into the tangled grey mess, while the softer brush held the skinny legs immobile as she stretched the web, twirling it strongly into the white nylon and yet pulling so lightly that only the very smallest of creatures would feel it as pulling. The web removed, the two united wings flapped frantically again. They didn't seem to have touched the lethal grey rope, but for all he flapped, they would not separate. He could not fly. So she had fed him.

After his long struggle and his long wait, the bee lay very still. She had no way of knowing if he had had enough syrup to generate his own energy, the last possible solution of the last problem. Well, said the voices cheerfully, in unison, I've done my best, and that's probably good enough. Maggie emptied the spoon into the grass-blades, wiped her brushes on the underside of a holly-bush, and went in, leaving him.

It would soon be time to put the light on. Perched on the high stool at the counter-top, she reached for the writing pad that lay open there, a coffee-stain on the top page, and wrote,

'Dear George, You say you want a separation, and probably a divorce, as it seems the only possible outcome of the mess things are in. On the whole, I agree with this, I think. I was annoyed when you wrote rather than telephone me, but in fact I've been doing a lot of thinking over the past five days. . .'

Briskly she wrote on, with the occasional pause for thought, when her head would lift, her hand stop, and her eyes travel measuringly around the kitchen as she evaluated, not what she wanted to say, for that was known, but how best to meet him as and where he was. It wasn't difficult, it simply required attention, and the voice that spoke through her pen was infinitely attentive to the stages of the task. It was during one of the pauses that her eye was caught by a large, dark, clumsy flying body outside the window. It was a bumble bee, travelling noisily, erratically, as bumble bees do, up towards the house eaves where the sun still faintly shone. Maggie smiled, and bent over her letter.

# THE SINK

*Jeff Torrington*

Curly Brogan had an idea: the bones of it was that he'd fake being dead.

'I like it so far,' I said.

We were lounging against the storage yard wall having a puff. A bright morning. Sun loose in the sky like a runaway cartwheel and tawny spokes of light glancing everywhere. Tarry odours rising from our spattered boilersuits. Out here nothing much doing in the way of work: the midget, Stacey, was forklifting car bodyshells onto the loading platform where a hoist gang leisurely transferred them to paint trolleys; over by the watertank the Sleeper was fixing up a cardboard-and-foam 'sunbed'.

Brogan scraped a blob of underseal from his forearm. Toad-like, lenses of sweat quickening in the rough folds of his face, and his baggy body leaking dank odours, he was not a man to get down-wind of. Most of the men kept him at arms' length, though they did send him to croak on their behalf at union meetings: Brogan was a croaker of distinction in that shrill swamp.

'What d'you think then?'

''Bout you being dead?' I took a saving drag on my skinny roll-up. The thought of this two hundredweight bag of dung dropping into a hole appealed to me. For a start, I'd no longer be plagued by the man's brute stinks – his 'after-grave' lotion, as the men called it. Another boon would be not having to listen to all that Marxian fart Brogan was forever braying. If there really was a spectre haunting Europe, then one whiff from Brogan's armpit would soon exorcise it. On the other hand, as shop-rep the man was really indispensable. What other steward could strike terror into the Martians' nostrils at a distance of fifty yards? They trembled at the very tread of his unwashed feet. I took another half-draw on my fag. 'Tell me about it,' I invited.

It seemed that the man who'd the misfortune to rent the flat beneath Brogan's had been sent home to die. 'Liver's just like a chunk of cardboard,' Brogan explained. 'Alcoholic. Telling you, if they cremate'm he'll burn for a fortnight.'

With a scattering of blonde sparks my cigarette stub spun away. 'I'm still not with you.'

'Simple. The bloke I'm on about has the same monicker as me. You maybe remember 'm – worked in the Paint Shop 'bout two years back. No relation mind, but the same name 'n address. Time clerk was always getting our cards arsy-versy. Pay office as well. Get it now?'

I nodded. 'Just about. When this neighbour of yours pegs out, say today or tomorrow, it'll get around it's you, right?' The other nodded. 'Then, I suppose, there'll be a notice in the snuffer columns, and that'll put the tin lid on it.'

'Pine lid's more like it.' Brogan dropped his cig-butt and heel-screwed it. 'He'll be a goner by tonight. Tea's definitely out.' We watched the Sleeper trying out his 'sunbed', laying his long, stark body on the yellow foamrubber. A private plane with white lettering on its cherry body passed daintily overhead. The pilot, I mused, would think he was overpassing a car plant. But he wasn't. Beneath him was a mechanised madhouse, an industrial asylum where adults on the nightshift played kids' games like 'I Spy' or 'Filmstars', while, here on the dayshift, they found amusement in pretending to be dead.

'What's the point?' I asked him.

Brogan showed pitted teeth. 'Come Friday night, there's Spunky Madden's stag-party . . . Think of their faces when yours truly shows up in a double-breasted shroud.'

'You'd lose three days money for that?'

'Worth three weeks. Anyway, I told you, I'm down for leave-of-absence for the boy's wedding in Torquay.'

The Sleeper hid his 'sunbed' behind some oildrums then walked stiffly across the yard towards us. 'Get a smash at that,' Brogan said as he jammed his cap on his brutally cropped head. 'A bloody bolt through his neck, that's all he needs.' We nodded to the bleak giant but he passed us as if we were stains on the wall and vanished into the building.

We followed a few minutes later, walking beneath the Widow where it formed a loop to carry its paper-shrouded car bodies from the undersealing booth then along the de-masking grid. The burdened cradles rocked as they negotiated the tight bend and from the cars' freshly-sprayed undersides a black rain fell on the tarpapered floor. Before ducking into The Hole I paused to tighten the muslin rag about my neck, jockeyed the mouth-mask into position, then pulled up my boilersuit hood. I took the gun from the relief man who moved quickly away, glad no doubt to get out of the tarry tomb of the underseal booth. I spent every minute of every hour in there wishing exactly the same thing. With the underseal pumps behind me beating out their unflagging rhythm I took up my spraying position, feet apart, head held up and slightly tilted backwards, a stance which eventually played hell with the old dorsal system. An estate car body closed over my head like a lid. I raised the gun's nozzle and with sweeping motions began to spray the tape-festooned underside with sealer.

Through the booth's tarry slit I could see Brogan jawing to a trimline steward. As a demasker Brogan had one of the cushiest numbers in the squad, his job being to merely rip off the masking tape that'd been slapped over boltholes and other orifices to prevent underseal fouling them. The steward moved away (maybe he was getting short on oxygen) and Brogan continued to crop masking tape, dropping it in fouled lumps into a wastebin. There was no doubt of it, the man was a boil on the world's backside. But maybe that made the world more careful about who or what it sat on. Brogan, hooking into my gaze, grinned down at me. He raised a gauntleted hand to his chest then making his short legs wobble he mimicked a heart-attack. I laughed at his antics but nevertheless I was telepathing to him this deadly serious wish: Go down for real, you bastard. Go down for real and let me out of here . . .

That night I'd a dream in which Brogan, armed with a torn butterfly net, went staggering through a grove of turpentine trees that showered him with a hot black resin. He was chasing a cherry-coloured moth with tiny death-heads etched on its wings, but it kept fluttering a yard or so ahead of his uselessly swooping net. The moth changed into a humming bird which lured him into a quicksand then hovered above his slowly disappearing head while it uttered strange flute-like notes. I felt an elbow in my back as I groaned awake. 'Who can it be at this time of night?' my wife asked. She'd switched on the bedside lamp and I sat up with hurting eyes. A slimy cough began to unwind in my chest as I reached for the chirruping telephone.

'Hullo?'

Brogan's voice boomed in my ear. 'That's some bark you've got – should see a vet.'

I frowned. 'D'you know what time it is?'

Brogan chuckled. 'What's time to a deader?'

'You pissed or something?'

There was a swallowing sound followed by Brogan's heavy breathing. 'Just a wee rehearsal for the boy's wedding.' The voice changed. 'Listen, I'm giving you this bell to let you know everything's fixed.'

'Fixed?'

'That's right. Just fall in line. Hullo? You still there?'

Another conversation had broken into the circuit and eventually collided with Brogan's to produce a pile-up of wrecked sentences . . . Hullo . . . who's there? . . . is that you, Malcolm? . . . get off the line . . . funeral . . . I'm trying to . . . stag party . . . hello . . .'

I clamped down the receiver then lifted it again and dropped it on the bedside table. I dragged back the covers and got out of bed. My wife spoke to me as I poked my feet into slippers: I shrugged. Nobody. Just a mate. Drunk. I went through to the bathroom and spat blackly into the sink, then I went downstairs for my roll-up tin.

The next morning, five minutes before the Widow stirred, I was standing by the cards table jazzing a teabag in my mug. I felt rough. I always felt rough at this a.m. Very growly. Knowing this most of the lads steered clear of me till after the first hour. What kind of life was it when you had to hype yourself up every morning to start work, to crawl into that funky black Hole and die a little more. No life at all. It couldn't go on, either that or I'd be into pills and booze like the rest of them, candidates for the long-sleeved jacket. The last person I needed at that moment was Gus Gebbie, but here was the man himself, coming at the trot into the section, bearing down on me. Gebbie was a small man, quick as an otter, with a frisky talent for surfacing from even the drabbest stream of events with a wriggling, juicy rumour in his mouth. Lies, exaggeration, distortion, innuendo, scandal – all were as natural to this man as were lumps to canteen custard. So expert was he in the art of fact-bending that anyone in the plant judged to be tarting up the truth would hear the time-honoured phrase – Don't come the Gebbie! It was a safe bet that if the Martians wanted a rumour leaked onto the shopfloor they would tell their agent: Get this to Gebbie. Now, his morning face alive with news, he came pattering up to me. 'I suppose you've heard,' he began.

'Shag off, Gus.'

Gebbie, as usual, was unabashed. 'It's about Curly,' he said.

I slung the sapped teabag into a bin. 'What about'm?'

'He's a goner. Cerebral haemorrhage. His brother phoned me last night.'

The news of Brogan's death, accelerated by Gebbie's genius, was all over the plant in an hour: from underseal to paint shop, and from there into the body-in-white, and the press shop, it hummed like black electricity, penetrating the tool room, the steel store, and on the back of the Widow into the main assembly block where it ran in thrilling tributaries into the axle section, the wheels and tyres, gearbox section, and engine drop-point. It even reached 'Siberia', the sales compound, where misty denizens could be seen from afar checking out – so the rumour went – birds' nests in the unsold car section.

I was in the pump area hooking up a fresh barrel of underseal when Tombstone Telfer, the section's greyback, approached. A man who believed smiling caused cancer, he came today with just a glimmer of gladness on his thin lips. He carried a crewsheet pinned to a clipboard and I was quick to note that Brogan's name had been scored through in thick black ink: it was not hard to imagine with what malicious joy Telfer had made that stroke.

At first handling conversations about Brogan's 'death' had been a botheration. All those crappy sayings as they dropped from this or that mouth: He'll be missed . . . can't get over it . . . looked as strong as a puggy . . . you never know the minute . . . had irked me. But after an hour or so attitudes began to normalise. 'I hear,' said big Tam Guyler with that side-mouthed drawl of his, 'that Curly's undertaker's claiming "dirty money".' Someone else had it about that the local sewage works was already flying its flag at half-mast. There was also a story to the effect that when the priest heard that it was Curly Brogan he was going to see, he'd tried to phone in the Last Rites.

'Leave that,' Telfer commanded, and moving on indicated with a choppy head-signal that I was to follow him. Walking a pace or so behind the greyback I met up with the Irish Sweep, a brusher-up whose brain, it was said, was being mailed to him by instalments. 'Is that right about Curly?' he asked. When I confirmed it he shuffled his big grey boots and said: 'I hear it was a terrible haemorrhage.'

'A cerebral haemorrhage, Eddie.'

'Aye, terrible right enough . . .'

Aware of Telfer's impatience I moved on. I received a few friendly waves from the seat-builders in the carousel section and Naughton, the mute, over in the repairs bay mimed his knowledge of Brogan's demise by holding his nose then drawing a finger across his throat. The greyback led me, as I'd expected, to The Byre, an office near the Snack Area which always looked too fragile to house the ferocious personality of Ted Bullock. As we went into the office Bullock was making one of his theatrical phone 'bawls', punching words into somebody's eardrum as if his mouth was a nailgun. Brogan claimed that this was a show to intimidate shop stewards or even greybacks, and that in reality he was yelling down an empty line. Whichever it was, he was good at it. There were other psychological props, such as the rickety chair I was being waved towards (contrast it with the king-sized, upholstered job Bullock was lording it in) or the photograph of Bullock himself, receiving a warm handshake from the Supreme Martian at a Paris motor show; another touch was the large blue ashtray on the boss-side of the desk compared with the coffee-jar lid I'd to make do with.

The phone receiver made its expected crash-landing in the cradle. The Bull now addressed a few remarks to the greyback about the availability of velour seat covers; then, after running a finely pointed pencil down figure columns on a print-out, he very gradually brought me into focus. 'Sorry to hear about Brogan,' he said, lounging back in his ritzy chair. 'How old was he?' When I told him, he cocked an eyebrow. 'Took'm for fifty at least.' He stroked his silvery hair. 'It's this place – puts years on you . . .' The patter went on in all its phoniness for a few minutes more – hypocrisy humming to itself at the graveside, masking its smirk with a hankie. It was funny to remember that the subject of all this fakery was probably sitting half-smugged in a Torquay-bound train.

'Listen, John,' the Bull said affably (though incorrectly, for my first name's Frank), 'this business leaves one or two things up-in-the-air. Now the way I see it . . .' I interrupted him and he held up an acknowledging hand. 'Yes, I accept that but this is purely informal. At the moment you're a deputy shoppy, right. And, so I hear, once you've had a meeting with the lads it's on the cards they'll elect you their steward. Right, good – let's take it from there. Tell you what I'm after . . .'

And he did, while I let his words drift through my head. Brogan's hoax was becoming like that variety act in which the performer sets a whole series of plates spinning on rods then dashes from one to the other to preserve its motion. It was obvious that sooner or later some part of the joke was going to wobble out of control, then the entire farce would come crashing down. The Bull droned on. What he was after was peace and harmony in the underseal section. Certainly, Mr Brogan had only been doing his job but recently things had got so tight that, well, a sparrow couldn't shit on the underseal roof without a Block meeting being called. Things had become too tight. It was time to end the confrontation . . . At this I sat up a little. Could I perhaps sniff a deal in the air?

Later that afternoon I was sitting in the trimshop snack area having a smoke and a coffee. It was a rowdy spot: there was the usual din from the nearby seats section; the gruff horns of forklift trucks as they plied to and fro in the passageways; and, closer at hand, the gab of men enjoying a respite from the tracks. At my elbow, Spunky Madden was doing one of his card tricks and a group of spectators was craning over him watching every move. I was well-used to Madden's jiggery-pokery and watched his card manipulations with only mild interest. I glanced up. Two senior stewards, Ron Yardley and the portly Alf Cross, were nodding to me as they approached. They sat down and lit fags. Yardley grinned (Cross didn't) at the chirrups from the adjacent tables. 'Watch it, lads – it's Trotsky and Potsky. Must be important, they're effin moving . . .'

Cross, whose nickname 'Double' was a well-known sarcasm, wasted little time in coming to the point. Scarcely allowing Yardley more than a minute to lay a small verbal wreath for Brogan – A good man to have on your side . . . got mucked into the Martians . . . dependable – he leaned aggressively towards me. 'I hear you were in The Byre this morning.' I nodded. 'The Bull crying on your shoulder 'bout Curly, was he?' Cross wasn't bothering to conceal his dislike for me. His cigarette died with a hiss in a coffee puddle. 'Or maybe he was trying you out for size in his back pocket.'

Yardley, who looked faintly embarrassed by his partner's vehemence, tapped some fag ash into a plastic coffee cup. 'We hear you've got Curly's job already. 'S'that right?' (My, the T & G tom-toms had been busy.)

I flipped the lid from my roll-up tin and began to tear out some rust shag. 'The job goes with the territory, you should know that. Makes it easier to get to union meetings and so on.'

'Well don't be getting any ideas of becoming the section's shoppy,' Cross said.

'That's up to the men, surely.'

Cross shook his head. 'Vic Logan's the man for the job.'

I grinned. Obviously they hadn't done their homework. 'Logan's on the mirror-shift. How can he be . . .'

'He's swopping over with Spunky Madden,' said Yardley. He dropped his fag butt into his empty coffee cup. 'No disrespect to yourself, Frank, but what we need now's a really experienced shoppy. Y'see, when a new steward happens along the Martians usually dish out the lollipops. You know, to sweeten him up. That's why it's a good time to screw a favour from the buggers.'

'I already have,' I said. I ran my tongue along the adhesive strip of the roll-up, then I massaged it into shape . . . 'D'you know what they're giving us?' Both men waited expectantly. When I told them, their jaws twitched.

'A sink,' Cross eventually said. 'A bloody sink!'

'With an electric urn,' I added as I tapped the loose shag into the ends of the roll-up. 'They're going to whip out the cracked sink we've got now'n replace it – top priority. We'll be able to wash-up in the section now. Never could get Curly interested.' I grinned. 'Well, you know what he thought about water.'

The stewards, slightly dazed-looking, left me. I watched them go then stuck the roll-up between my smiling lips. Spunky Madden nudged me then passed over a piece of paper. It was a cartoon, obviously from the hand of Leroy of the wet-deck. It showed Brogan's burial, the coffin surrounded by a crowd of mourners wearing gas-masks, the same applied even to the officiating priest who read the sermon from *Das Kapital*. Ghosts from adjacent plots could be seen whizzing off with packed suitcases, fingers held to their spectral noses. In the foreground a worm was saying to its partner: We've got a ripe one here!

I laughed and returned the drawing to Madden. It was shortly after this that Donny Morton from the inspection booth came with the good news that the facilities men were already in the underseal section checking out the new sink's location. 'You're some kid, eh?' said Spunky Madden. 'Brogan for stinks – Frankie boy for sinks!'

I was standing by my locker the next morning, getting into my boilersuit, when Vic Logan, the nightshift rep, came up to me. Usually good for a joke, even after a ten-hour stint, Logan looked sombre this morning. He'd something important to tell me but he wouldn't discuss it in the locker room. At Logan's request I agreed to go with him to the loading bay. On our way there, as we skirted around the paint trollies that cluttered the floor, I got a pleasant surprise: for the first time in the history of the Centaur Car Company, a plumber had actually been working on the nightshift, a rebuff to those cynics who claimed that the nocturnal leak-brigade spent the dark hours beneath an upturned tub playing at Brag. The old sink, its back broken, lay like a set of enormous dentures on the floor, and its stainless steel replacement was already bolted to the wall.

'The sparks'll be here today to stick in the urn,' Logan said, though it was obvious by his tone that he'd other things on his mind. On the loading bay we lit cigarettes. Beneath the platform in the grey yard there was the noisy going and coming of workers, nightshift flowing through dayshift and, beyond this intermingling, the frantic bleating of horns from the car park.

Sometimes, for the squad's amusement, Spunky Madden put on a lunchtime conjuring show. Eggs turned into apples, paper flowers volleyed from empty soup cans, coins were snatched from the air. And all of this mystification unfurled on a stream of patter without which, it seemed, the machinery of the con would seize up and spit out its dry bearings. This very calamity was happening now as Logan's words were blasted by the 'man-your-stations' klaxon. I strained to hear.

'The snipes found what?'

'Two car radios,' Logan repeated.

'Where?'

'I told you – in Curly's locker.'

It turned out an anonymous caller had phoned plant security to report that stolen property was to be found in Curly Brogan's locker. With independent witnesses present the snipes had opened Curly's locker and found the radios wrapped in an old boilersuit at the bottom.

'The silly bastard,' was all I could find to say. I kept repeating the words over and over while my fierce draws on the cigarette sowed sparks in the gloom. Out in the yard the last few stragglers were making their way into their respective buildings. Through the wall I could hear the underseal pumps starting up.

'I supose they'll raid his house,' Logan said. 'Even although the poor sod's snuffed it.'

I nodded. The snipes would go all the way to Hell for a wind-screen wiper. It was on the cards, too, that they'd raided the wrong flat – went stampeding into the dead Brogan's gaff waving their bloody search warrant. You get the coffin, Charlie, I'll frisk the widow. Well, it would all come out in the wash now. And nothing to be done for Brogan. Nothing. A bagging case pure and simple. Brogan, himself, never defended a thief; just pulled the plug on him. He could expect nothing different.

Later, as I stripped tape from the undersealed cars and chucked the soiled croppings into the bin, doing this over and over again until my brain eventually switched into auto-pilot and my mind was free to wander, I recalled something Brogan had read aloud to me from one of his lefty books: 'The Capitalists are the tomb-robbers of history. They steal forth in the night to breach that door behind which Democracy sleeps its ill-fated sleep. And not content with having slain it they now lay their avaricious hands upon it and strip it to the very bones . . .' I can't remember how the rest went but how ironically apt that quotation was although quite the reverse had happened to him, hadn't it. By posing dead he had invited the attention not of a tomb-robber but of a name-eraser; some malicious person or persons had, it seemed, stolen forth in the night to . . .

The hooter sounded and the Widow stopped. As I came down off the ramp Spunky Madden came from The Hole, unwinding his neck-gauze and pushing back his boilersuit hood. He looked sweaty and half-knackered and I knew for certain that his back would be louping. 'You're wanted,' he said, and taking me by the elbow led me towards the loading bay. Most of the squad had assembled there and there was a lot of jocular remarks flung in my direction as Madden led me into their midst. 'Clear the way, lads,' Madden said and the crowd parted to reveal the gleaming sink, complete with hot-water urn, although this hadn't been connected yet. Spunky handed me a small bar of soap. 'Right, Frank, do us the honours.'

I grinned and stepped up to the sink. I turned on the tap and a robust gush of water soused the steel. Dipping my hands into the flow I palpated the soap. Spunky Madden began to laugh. The others joined him, their hilarity soon swelling with derision as with a soft oath I sheepishly turned and held aloft my black stained hands.

# THE MEAT

*Janice Galloway*

The carcass hung in the shop for nine days till the edges congested and turned brown in the air.

People came and went. They bought wafers of beef, pale veal, ham from the slicer, joints, fillets, mutton chops. They took tomatoes and brown eggs, tins of fruit cocktail, cherries, handfuls of green parsley, bones. But no one wanted the meat. It dangled overhead on a claw hook, flayed and split down the spinal column: familar enough in its way. It was cheap. But it did not attract. Instead, they asked for shin and oxtail, potted head, trotters. The meat refused to sell. Folk seemed embarrassed even to be caught keeking in its direction. One or two made tentative enquiries about a plate of sausages, coiled to the left of the dangling shadow, while the yellowing hulk hung restless, twisting on a spike. These were never followed through. The sausages sat on, pink and greasy, never shrinking by so much as a link. He moved the sausages to another part of the shop where they sold within the hour. Something about the meat was infecting.

By the tenth day, the fat on its surface turned leathery and translucent like the rind of an old cheese. Flies landed in the curves of the neck and he did not brush them away. The deepset ball of bone sunk in the shoulder turned pale blue. There was no denying the fact: it had to be moved. The ribs were sticky and the smell had begun to repulse him, clogging the air of the already clammy interior of the shop, and he could detect its unmistakable seep under

37

the door to his living-room when he was alone in the evening. So he fetched the stool and reached out to the lard hook, seized the meat and, with one accurate slice of the cleaver, cut it down. It languished on the sawdust floor till nightfall, then he threw it into the back close that ran parallel to the street. As he closed the shutter on the back door, he could hear the scuffling of small animals and strays.

In the morning, all that remained was the hair and a strip of tartan ribbon. These he salvaged and sealed in a plain wooden box beneath the marital bed. A wee minding.

# OG'S FEE

*Brian Mitchell*

It was a three-oh of us as (I) remember; all niners and as good friendbefair kids as ever ganged abroad in the New Territorious Domain; as ever hushtrod the bare brown parths feeling quick and slight where the girt, peduncular feet of trees sank under, horny and greened; as ever boastbartered in the rutted wake of precentury carts, or lingered hay-hearted in the cool of rootshade. Anyway, the sky that day stood like a huge, unimportant door shut happily on heaven, and the grass grew rank and clear as jewelreed, glinting and buzzing in the weight of the sun, as the lane took us and turned us and emptied for our guidance all its corners and pockets and unsuspected stations, all completely out.

Three of us, they were; all scruffed together in rayment of innocence, their young cores jackfurred with the pelt of adventure (me behind my glasses a bit, but), all agame, as wise as cubs and clean as pebbles, progressing like corpuscles along a deep integral lein which wound ever inward to the brooding green heartseat of that wild land. They didn't know, there being the whole of rebellious nettledom to subdue, an ammunificence of stones for re-location, unlimited ours, how near they were (a hedgedepth, a wing's-wind); yet, being that close, they knew – could sense – the intense explosiary of Being raging silently cell by cell; the billions of patient leaves . . . the thickening of gnarl and hull . . . the blizzard-ous launching of tiny sad insects and dry, sleepstuffed seeds.

(Well, I can tell you that we all had pasts or else we couldn't have been there, but those were fading like summer mists – Pneumae Mortis, remembered only in the pitfalls of night.)

Birds flew in at the windows of trees, leaving their songs to plaint the air; they wove in and out of hedgesticks and perched askance on knotty sprigs. Some trees, taller even than houses, reached down to find again the dark burial earth with a blind, leaf-cumbered sinuosity of bough; others spiralled their branches through roomfuls of furnished air, fingering the shifting sunlight with transluminous leaves; while down on the fundal, weeds waist high and headhigher craned for the sunflood, trapping the plump laze of summer within the tough lizardous flesh of their pri-mal leaf. Great greenweb plates and spoked umbrellas, with snaking rootclumps laired in hidden ditches, and then . . . just hovering in the viridity . . . breathclouds of starry white flowers.

(Is something . . . ?)

Three fry, languidly lounging, peeling straitsticks for swords, their sporadically passionate chatter lagged and muted by air benign,

(. . . something coming?)

when, from their tri-headed absorption, one happened to glance up. He started.

. . . YES!

The others jerked round to follow his look and then all three were netted in a pall of exposure.

It was Og.

Naturally, out of the earth, out of its mad matted generations he had come. A giant. Of mud and beef, turnip-headed and sly-eyed, a louching local farmboy out for fun. He was not fat but as slow and compact as a bullock, dragging his deadleather boots through the dusty grass, thwarting the lane, and bearing in his clodlike hands a long gun.

The Giant squinted down at us, calculating in the blunt forelump of his brain what weight of tribute he would take that day.

## The Gun

It was more solid than anything in the world. The handle-end was like thick furniture, scratched somewhat and sweatdulled, but still a man's polished club, shaped to a torso like an artificial limb. The barrel was machined from cold killing iron; it poked hard and straight wherever it was pointed and every so often we saw the frightening, lazy black hole in the end. We all wondered who'd be first.

The Giant, grinning agrestically 'cross his frecklemole face, seemed to reach a conclusion. 'Bet you nippers 'an't never sin one o' these,' he challenged. His voice was still gruffly hooked to his Adam's apple and had ill-controlled moments when it scraped like rusty farm machinery.

''Course we have,' we stoutly lied from somewhere between the three of us.

'But you 'an't never *shot* one.'

And there he had us.

'I shoot all the time,' prided Og, importantly.

'What?' (We knew, but had to ask.)

'Anything I like.' And putting the gunstock to his heavy shoulder and screwing up his whole mass to sight along the barrel, he turreted round in a slow arc, aiming at all Creation but dipping specially low to be sure to include us. Seeing us back into each other in obvious alarm, he sniggered. ''Tarn't even loaded yet,' he ridiculed, 'But I've got lots o' slugs. See?' He groped fatfingered into his shirt pocket and then displayed to us on the pudge of his big palm a meddle of dull lead pellets. 'I like birds, mostly,' he told us.

Above the hemming wall of growth they sailed on motionless wings, higher than the string of any reach. At every point, above the tumult of verdurous struggle, they clung to slender branches and sang with the fullness of their puffpouch breasts, the way furnace-stokers shout dumbly into the roar of flames. They crept, ahop-aflutter, through the inner structure of brake and thicket; dug shyly for grubs in the crusts of trees.

'Wanna see me?' said Og to three fledgling boys on an over-grown farmtrack deep in the green flux of Nature's skin.

Og broke open the gun, revealing its flat, slidy gut, glistening lubriciously in the torpid air, and a small internal nostril, into which he sweatily thumbed a single pellet.

Og snapped the gun shut with a flinch of meaty arms, said a stern: 'shsh' to three who hardly breathed, then spat loudly into the grass at his feet.

I swear by every stone in the Bible I thought they were all safe. Search frantically as I did with the horrid sick tension in my stomach, I could not see a single one. Nor hear one, either. There was only the huge suffocating drowse and millions of waiting leaves, behind every one of which, perhaps, a wary creature was hiding its life.

But John Ogman had a special eye. Deadeye, it's called. As he scanned the nearby hedge, scowling with concentration, a change came over the land. The slow hydraulic welling of sap in hundreds of miles of branches stopped and solidified. The vulnerable, moistveined leaves grew skeletal then powdered away. Flowers became bleached and desiccated, and down! Down fell the fullness. Away blew the mystery, and all the wild loll of beauty drained into nothing. This all happened and there, right in the epicentre of the giant's eye, trapped in a cage of enclosing thorns, was a tiny bird. It was worse than winter for that poor wren; it was orphaned of everything that fed it life, its entire givenness . . .

Taken.

The gun hiccupped at something that slashed the hedgeleaves, there was a fractional squawk, a twiggy stumble, and –

'Got 'un,' shouted the exultant farmlad. 'See that? First go an' all.'

It was the grossness of his triumph that shocked, and the smirk of self-congratulation contorting his man's mouth that bred hatred, before we had really comprehended what we'd seen him do. It was those things that intimidated us and made us long to escape, but we knew somehow that our toll was not yet paid in full so we stood in awkward silence while our captor felt about in a pocket of the hedge and then drew something out with a satisfied grunt. 'There y'are, see.'

We had no choice but to look. The Giant held out in his discomforting fist the little creature he had killed instead of us; held it close up before each of us in turn.

### The Bird
Tombed in the padleather of the Giant's paw, spidery feet half curled, its breast an untidy ruffle of down and its eyes fiercely shut, it

slept stubbornly Death's hectic sleep, our burden of lead in its miniature heart.

None of us said a word but one of us was . . .

'Look at the li'l cissy,' roared the young bruteman, delighting in his own scorn. 'Crybaby. It's only a bird.'

To demonstrate its insignificance he gave the dead bird a contemptuous squeeze which made it look for a moment as though it was raising its head to sing. Then he flung it away among the weeds.

True enough, while there hadn't been a speck of blood on the bird – everthing about it being fixed, dry, and vacant – on this side of the glasses, as though vision itself were wounded, a stinging fluid seeped uncontrollably, shamefully, blurring and blotting the now sinister vegetation into a choking lye.

Which may be why the record is unclear whether it was Og himself, made suddenly taller and somehow governed by cynicism, or some Overvoice that had witnessed the whole affair

bound in resigning silence, and who only then
(and then so bitterly)
welcomed three more heirs-general
to the estate of Men.

# THE TAIRSGEIR

*Morag Henriksen*

'Someone has started cutting right next to our peats.'

'What! Where?'

'Along the old drain that runs into our bank.'

'Did you see them?'

'No. There was nobody there – just the cut peats. They're spread across our track to the stile.'

'What!' Mairi's voice was rising in pitch. Her blood was rising, too, in a way that surprised her. Instantly she felt threatened.

The peat-bank, about three miles out of the small town, was a place away from people – a sanctuary of peace, precious in its emptiness, its freedom from neighbourly intrusion. And someone was crowding in. A robin could not have felt more hostile to the intruder on its territory than she did.

'Have they cut much? Have they kept away from our spread?'

'Well, they've spread a bit on our side of the ditch,' her husband admitted. 'You'll see for yourself.'

They had planned to start cutting next day. It would be their fifteenth year at that bank. When they came to the island first from Glasgow, Mairi had shown Neil how to cut peats. It was part of her heritage; she had absorbed it from watching her father at work. Neil was a city lad but eager to learn. In those days very few people cut peats. All the locals were installing oil-fired central heating or proudly declaring themselves all-electric. Now, with money short and fuel prices rising, the hill-side was dotted with fresh peat-cuttings again.

Mairi was surprised at the strength of her feeling about the encroachment on their small piece of moor. They had permission to cut there from Cally MacLeod, the township clerk. It was his apportionment of the common grazing and sometimes his cattle wandered across the bog leaving hoof-marks and dung on the peats.

'The whole wide world to choose from and they have to crowd in on top of us!'

She had lost her peace of mind and lost it still further the next morning when Neil came back from skinning the bank, a job she could not do because the surface turves were too heavy for her to lift. 'Remember Murdo Stewart, the tinker boy, who was in that 3C class we both taught? Well, it's him and another of his relations who are cutting next to us.'

'Did you say anything to them? Did you ask if they had permission?'

'Well, no. What right had I to object? They've as much right to cut peats as we have.'

'Away you go! You're far too soft. You'd let anyone walk all over you.'

'I suppose I am. I just have this thing about other people's liberties.'

'At the expense of *our* liberties! Don't be daft!'

Mairi could hardly wait until Neil had taken his soup. She was spoiling for a fight. The violence of her feeling astonished her. She remembered words spoken late one night long ago. 'I'm basically a pacifist,' she had told her new husband, 'but I'll fight like a wildcat if anyone threatens my territory.'

They drove out to the bank at last and unloaded the car – thermos flask and biscuits, boots, a modern plastic ball-barrow and an old tairsgeir given to them by Hecky the Post, who had no more need of it. Every year he asked if it was all right. Its blade was honed away to a thin slip of iron; its wood had the patina of antiquity, steeped in bog acid, smoothed by years of labouring hands. Mairi loved using the tairsgeir; Neil used a spade.

From the road she could see the tinkers. They had moved away to a second bank at a slight distance. That one belonged to an uncle and obviously they were cutting for the whole family. There was an amazing wall of peats stacked at the edge of the new bank. Even in the midst of her irritation she could not help admiring its perfection. Every peat was the same as its neighbour. It was ruler straight and spaced like a soft brick wall with gaps for the wind to whistle through.

To get to the bank she had to stand on some of the newly cut peats. It went against the grain to do this. She resented having to spoil good peats; she resented the loss of freedom. The beaten path of fifteen years was quite obvious through the heather and flattened moss.

The first arrival at the moor was always a precious moment – had been a precious moment. The long strip of naked peat waited to be pared off in turves, the turves to be spread out on the heather to dry in the wind, then stood on end and propped in threes and fours to dry out completely before the harvest home to the peat-shed – all that lay ahead. There was the prospect of hours of hard work in the fresh air and the special freedom of the moor, the good exercise, the tranquillity and at last the reward of security and warmth in the winter to come.

Here and now at the top of the bank was nothing but aggravation. Neil had understated the situation. Not only was their access impeded but a large mass of peats covered the moor where the Murchisons needed to spread their crop. Empty breadwrappers blew in the wind.

Mairi bounded over the intervening heather to where the two Stewarts were bending and cutting, lifting and throwing turf rhythmically. Two small men, bonnets pulled low over their noses, tattered jerseys and dungarees. She towered over them, an Amazon in climbing boots. 'Did you get permission to cut that bank?' Her voice would have done the cutting for them. They knew trouble when they saw it and adopted defensive attitudes. They ignored her question.

'You are cutting far too close to our bank. You've blocked our path to the stile and you have spread your peats across our spread. We've been cutting here for fifteen years and never a bit of bother have we had in all that time until now.'

The older man blustered a little. 'We're not blocking your path at all.'

'Oh yes you are. Come and see. And *have* you got permission?'

'Yes. Cally said we could cut that old bank.' The younger Stewart obviously remembered his days in the classroom. He answered her meekly.

They strode across the bog to the Murchisons' bank and studied the problem.

'Now you see. That's our path covered with your peats and we usually spread all the way back up there where your peats are. If you'd kept to your side of the ditch and left us room to go through there would be no problem.' She did not mention the towering resentment she had of them being there at all, but it showed. Far more than the words she used, her manner dominated them all. She crackled with indignation; she was huge. Neil stood like a man in the middle distance.

The older tinker capitulated suddenly. 'Come on, Murdo. We'll shift them,' he sighed.

'Good!' She turned her back on them to hide her relief and gazed across the small river to the ridge of hills. Neil began to skin the bank, the Stewarts to trudge to and fro moving peats further and further away.

She felt sorry for them and their additional labour, quite sympathetic now that she had won the day, but made no offer to help. It was their affair.

There was usually a heron in the stream or some ravens carking on the crags or even the cuckoo, but nothing called today. The moor was not the same any more.

She was urgent to begin working now so she took up the peat-iron and made the first slanting incision. Gradually the sods piled up, a tumble of glistening slabs. Mairi began to lay them out in neat rows below the cut bank. They did not get so much wind there but she did not feel like waiting for the tinkers to finish. She had to be doing something.

The Stewarts worked quietly and steadily, murmuring to each other in their own particular Gaelic. Eventually they had cleared a reasonable area, then meekly they enquired, 'Will that be enough, do you think?'

Mollified, she nodded. 'Yes. I think we'll manage at that but you'll need to clear the path too. We can't get past.'

They obeyed, tossing the peats further out onto the heather and replacing the batten of driftwood across the ditch.

'Ach, it's not a very good batten, this,' said one.

'Damned cheek!' thought Mairi. 'They're getting cocky again.'

'You shouldn't have put your first cut down on the bottom of the bank,' Murdo advised her.

This was too much. 'I know that!' she snapped. 'I'd have put them on the high bank if you'd left me a place to put them.'

They said no more until the track was cleared. 'Will that do now?'

'Yes. That'll be fine. Thanks.'

And, 'Thanks', Neil echoed from the far end of the peat-bank.

The work progressed peacefully. Cut and lift, cut and lift, cut and lift and throw. Neil could carry a few turves at a time on his spade. Mairi threw hers into the ball-barrow and trundled it across the wiry tussocks to lay out the neat rows which gradually covered over the heather and lichen and moss.

Cutting peats is back-breaking, boring and repetitive. It leaves your mind free to wander. Normally Mairi switched off mentally and listened to the small sounds of the moor, the burn, the ravens, the skylarks. Now and then the monotony would be broken by a toot and a wave from a passing car, somebody local going shopping in Ronavaig, acknowledging the fact that they were back at the peats. Often tourists stopped. Their ways are many and strange. They stalk a picture, turning the workers into aborigines to be snapped up and taken captive to holiday albums in Surbiton or Strasbourg. They pretend they are scanning the hills then snatch a quick photograph and scuttle back to their cars.

Today there were plenty of tourists. It was Bank Holiday weekend. The Murchisons watched them covertly, amused as always. A woman slammed on her brakes, leaned out and shot them straight into the sun. A flashlight bulb popped.

'Good life! What did she need that for?'

'She probably doesn't know how to work the camera without it.'

'The Stewarts make far better local colour than we do.'

'Yes. They look just right in the landscape. They blend. We may have been here first but they're indigenous.'

Over the heather all afternoon came the smell of fag-smoke and the noise from the tinkers' transistor – the frenetic gabble of a football commentator coming and going on the breeze. The skylarks gave up in disgust. When the footballers were exhausted they switched to a cassette. Hebridean Hawaii treacled across the moor.

'What has happened to me? I'm not as irritated as I usually am by that sort of pollution,' thought Mairi. 'Maybe Neil's live and let live philosophy is getting through to me. Or most likely it's because I got the better of them so I can afford to feel magnanimous.' In actual fact the Stewarts sharing their landscape were giving her fresh, lively channels of thought and she was enjoying herself.

Neil and Mairi took their thermos of coffee down to the bank of the burn and lay awhile basking in the sun.

'My back's getting a bit sore. Is yours?'

'Yes. I'm stiff. It's all the bending. Never mind. We'll have a day off tomorrow since it's Sunday. Can't cut peats on the Sabbath.'

'It's funny that. I thought I'd got rid of most of these taboos from my childhood, but that's one I cannot break. I don't even want to. Yet I bought some peas to put in the garden tomorrow. Why can I break the Sabbath planting peas and not cut peats?'

'Because it's one of the last vestiges of the old traditional way of life, that's why.'

'I suppose so. And gardening isn't . . .'

A caterpillar looped lost along her trouser-leg and she helped it onto a sprig of myrtle.

When they returned to their bog, the Stewarts watched them arrive and start cutting. They conferred and then began to walk purposefully towards them.

'Now what?' Mairi wondered, feeling no trouble in the air.

'Is everything all right now?' they asked in soft voices. 'Have you enough room?'

It was a peace mission and it was received amicably. 'Yes. I think we'll manage.'

'We wouldn't have got our peats mixed up anyway. They're a different pattern to yours.' Mairi surveyed her peats ruefully. Pattern was hardly the word. No two were the same. 'Right enough. Ours are all shapes and sizes. We've been admiring your beautiful wall. How did you get it so perfect?'

Admitting your own inadequacies takes away the power of your opponent's critical thought. 'Och, it's just the different shape of our peat-iron. Mine has a wider shaft and a shorter blade. Let me see yours a minute.'

Mairi handed up the tairsgeir and the tinker handled it briefly then gave it back.

'We haven't much space so we had to build the wall. They don't dry so well that way.'

'It looks really splendid though and it ought to catch the wind.'

'You're sure you have plenty of room?'

They hadn't but concessions had to be made. 'Yes. It should be all right.'

The overture was at an end. The men returned to their work. Two seconds later the head fell off the tairsgeir.

Mairi gazed at it in utter astonishment. So firmly had the iron shoe and the aged smoothed wood been melded together that they seemed all of a piece. It had never even wobbled, yet the head had just slid off the shaft like butter off a hot knife.

Neil came and fiddled with it. Overpoweringly Mairi wanted to hide it. She did not want the tinkers to see their triumph. Their triumph? What was this? 'Do you think they put the buisneach on the tairsgeir?'

'The evil eye? Is that what you think?' Neil looked at her in astonishment. He seemed to have been doing nothing else all day.

'Well, it's very funny, isn't it, that as soon as he touched it it fell apart.'

'You don't believe that, do you?'

'I don't know. I just don't know.'

'He didn't wrench it, did he?'

'No. You saw him yourself. He held it very lightly and gently and sort of stroked the blade.'

'Well it's no use now. You'd better go home and get a bit stick to wedge the head back on again. There's nothing else you can do.'

Mairi carried the broken peat-iron back to the car. She did not look near the tinkers. Conviction was growing in her that now the honours were even. They would be satisfied too. But the educated veneer of her stood aghast at such deep-rooted primitive superstition.

She thought hard as she drove back down to Ronavaig. She had to accept that the two were one. The primitive and the modern existed side by side in her just as in the tinkers. They threw litter about and played their horrible tinny tranny out of doors, yet they belonged to the landscape and made peat-cutting an art.

She had a university education and a city husband but her acquired sophistication had no power against the awareness in her of more primitive forces.

Mairi laughed suddenly. Her spirits soared. She was glad the tinkers had scored one back on her, that the skirmish had ended in a draw. She pulled into a passing-place and leaned out of the window. The moor was smiling again, shimmering in the sunlight, and high on Creagan Uaine the cuckoo called.

# ANYTHING IN TROUSERS
## William Oliphant

Wattie spent a whole week in the tailoring trade. It was never quite clear whether, when he left it, he was lured by the promise of a job in engineering or driven away by the laughter and the knowing looks of the two benches of trouser machinists vociferously led by Big Maud Tighe. One of life's natural enthusiasts, he had certainly liked the idea of going to work in the clothing factory, and his last day at Inglis' shop had been spent in a stew of impatience.

'I'll be looking for a suit of clothes wholesale when you become a journeyman,' remarked Daddy Inglis as he paid Wattie the last wage he was to earn as a newspaper boy.

Wattie, who thought a journeyman must be some kind of travelling salesman and was therefore puzzled by the allusion, nevertheless assumed the man-to-man air he regarded as appropriate to one about to enter the great world of commerce and manufacture.

'No doubt something can be arranged, Mr Inglis,' he said. 'I'm thinking of taking up the pipe, and I'd expect my tobacconist to be decently dressed.'

The pseudo-parental pat on the head that Daddy Inglis was wont to bestow threatened to become a clout on the ear, but Wattie was off. He joined Billy on the pavement outside and they crossed towards Black Street.

'An old Jessie!' Wattie said. 'We should have called him Granny Inglis.'

'Ach! He's not a bad old stick,' Billy protested; but Wattie had ceased to listen. Again he bubbled over in anticipation of the new job.

'I'm fairly looking forward to Monday,' he enthused. 'Bags of machinery; and you should see the dames: thousands of them.'

As a description of the factory floor of S. Rose & Co., Clothing Manufacturer, Dobbies Loan, this was neither complete nor accurate. It would have taken a lot more than the brief glimpse Wattie had been given, during his interview with Mr Levine, to enable him to paint a more detailed picture. In fact, he wheeled many a skepful of pieces out of the cutting room and distributed them among the long benches of machinists before the first impression of a vast, organic body of noise resolved itself into separate cells of sound, and the pervasive odour of the place became recognisable as the compound of many individual smells.

Noise and smell; these were the first and most apparent characteristics of the factory. It produced clothing – jackets, waistcoats, trousers – and it did so with a screaming roar that spun your head, and in a stench that nauseated you, unless you were an old hand and had allowed two of your senses to be blunted beyond awareness; or unless you were a very new hand like Wattie who, from sheer enthusiasm, was able to listen through the noise and sniff beyond the smell.

The basic, underlying rumble, he discovered, was generated by the motor-driven shafts which ran between the pairs of benches and transferred motion by belt to machine. These gave off the smell of power: cold steel, warm bearings, hot oil, balata, vulcanite. The whirring was a hundred seams run up on a hundred sewing machines, the snipping, a hundred threads cut by a hundred pairs of scissors. The vinegary smell was from the dressing used in pocket linings and the buckram that was sewn as stiffening into trouser flies, waistbands and jacket fronts. The clack-clack-clack was the sound of the buttonholer, and the sustained buzz was the band knife cutting cloth, and when the cloth was Harris Tweed, the smell was peat. The steam irons and the Hoffman presses thumped and hissed and filled the air with the aroma of wet wool. And over all, the incessant waves of female conversation, and the vaguely acrid odour of sweating, female bodies.

As much as anything else, Wattie enjoyed the singing. One of the older women, as she worked at her machine, would be humming away at 'The Rose of Tralee' or 'Love's Old Sweet Song' when, first her own bench, then the entire floor would take it up, and for a time the noise of the machinery would be drowned in sweetness and harmony. As he aimed his laden skep up the narrow passage that ran along the ends of the benches, and threw bundles of 'stock' and 'specials' onto the checker's tables, Wattie found himself breathing the sentimental old songs. He knew them well, for his mother loved the music hall and was a good kitchen soprano to boot. He himself went a lot to the pictures, so he was also no stranger to the numbers the younger machinists sang. Under his breath he was Bing Crosby in 'The Blue of the Night' and could do a surreptitious Nelson Eddy to 'Rosemarie' and 'The Indian Love Call'.

The two end benches, the trouser machinists, were great for the singing, and in this, as in all else, it was Big Maud Tighe who took the lead. Big Maud had a glorious voice. A description of it was, more or less, a description of Maud herself: large, untutored, unrefined, but warm and with a laugh in it; a sort of gallus contralto. She could community-sing with the best of them; but when Chrissie McGarrity or Theresa MacIvor addressed her specifically ('Give us a song, Maud'), it was her extensive repertoire of bawdy ballads they were referring to, and it was with one of those that Maud would oblige.

'I am a Dundee weaver and I come frae bonnie Dundee.
I met a Glesga fella and he came coortin me.
He took me oot a-walkin doon by the Broomielaw,
And then the dirty wee rascal took my thingummyjig awa'.'

Her audience would take up the repeat of the last line, their scissors beating out the tempo on the tops of their machines: 'And then the dirty wee rascal took my thingummyjig awa'.'

It was usually at about this point in the proceedings that Mr Levine appeared, particularly if the girls were engaged on 'specials' he wanted out in a hurry. He bounced up and down the lines of benches creating, more than ever, the impression that he was in a perpetual state of sweaty excitement.

'No singing,' he squeaked. 'No talk, work hard, no singing.'

The import of Big Maud's reply was lost on him as he disappeared like a corpulent rabbit back into his cubby-hole of an office.

'Away and dally up a lamp post!' she cried.

A long life spent immured in clothing sweatshops had confirmed Mr Levine in a profound ignorance of the human female in general and the female machinist in particular. All machinists, he was convinced, had two attributes in common: they were mad, and they were lazy. Some of them were also coarse, lascivious, criminal, weak-minded, malicious, man-mad or money-mad or both or some or all of these things. It was necessary, at any rate, for him to appear in the midst of them periodically and exhort them to greater efforts. He was wrong about this. These girls were on piece work and inspection was meticulous. To make a living they had to keep their heads down. Maud was probably one of the best trouser machinists in the factory. She regularly lifted thirty-five shillings a week, and at eighteenpence per pair of trousers she was slinging no lead. Actual relaxation, in spite of the singing, was unknown until the power was switched off for the tea break.

It was Moosie Broon, a fifteen-year-old with three months more service than Wattie, who warned him about the tea break and the effects of relaxation on the two end benches, and of the dangers confronting uninitiated new boys caught in their vicinity with the power off. He had a fund of horrific tales, many of them no doubt apocryphal, of naked legs seen kicking frantically over the edges of empty skeps, of backsides with a lipstick-painted eye on each buttock, of trousers forcibly removed and returned later with the leg holes stitched across and a patch fitted over the fly button holes. Some of his descriptions were so lurid that Wattie was frankly sceptical.

'It takes a right sissy to let a few dames work a flanker on him.'

'Don't you believe it,' advised the sagacious Moosie. 'When there's about twelve of them holding you down, it wouldn't matter supposing they were midgets; and anyway, have you seen Big Maud? She's got muscles like Johnny Weissmuller. She could eat you for tea break and spend the rest of the morning spitting the seeds out between her teeth.'

'Like to see her try,' said Wattie.

Brave words, and of course, apprehensive though he might be, they had to be reinforced by demonstrations of temerity. Besides, there was a certain fascination in flouting danger, and an excitement in the thought that, at any moment, real women might hurl themselves upon him and bear him to the ground with their real arms and their real legs and their real breasts. However, they were, after all, only dames, and in the duelling which ensued each time he delivered trouser stock to the checker's table, he held his own.

'Aw! It's my own wee darlin' Wattie.' This was Chrissie McGarrity. 'Hows about you and me gettin' married?'

'I'm sorry, madam,' said Wattie solemnly. 'I promised first refusal to Big Maud.'

'I'll "Big Maud" you,' cried Big Maud. 'Less of your cheek or I'll have your guts for garters.'

'My favourite position,' said Wattie, manoeuvring his empty skep for getaway. 'Halfway up to heaven.'

Big Maud laughed as heartily as everyone else on the bench at Wattie's Parthian shot, but there was an air of finality in the way she spoke when the laughter died away.

'Right, girls,' she announced. 'It's the bottle treatment for that one. Remember now, first tea break he's up this way.'

And the very next day was Wattie's Waterloo. He made the tactical error of being caught with an armful of unmade trousers at the checker's table when the power went off for tea break. The factory suddenly became a squealing, female chaos full of bulging cotton overalls, smooth legs and spiky heels, broad hips, strong arms, coloured hair, and all the world's weight of women pinning him like paralysis to the floor. He felt rough hands upon his trouser flies and the shock of his flesh being inserted into the cold, narrow neck of a glass bottle.

'It's not coming up.' The distant voice was Chrissie McGarrity's.

'I'll fix that,' said Big Maud. She stood over Wattie, one foot at each side of his head. 'How's that for a view?' she bawled, and she slowly sank down on her knees until her great, fleshy thighs almost touched his face.

'It's rising, it's rising,' cried Chrissie McGarrity; but at that moment the air was pierced by a terrible scream, and Big Maud hurled herself away from Wattie's supine figure like a rock from a Roman ballista.

'The wee bugger's bit me!' she yelled.

The hands that held Wattie loosened in surprise. He shook them off, scrambled to his feet, tucked in semmit, shirt, bottle and all, and ran for it. A blur of laughing, female faces lined his path, his every step was derisively echoed by a hundred pairs of scissors rapped on a hundred bench tops. The factory acknowledged him.

'By Jesus, Maud!' said Chrissie McGarrity. 'Tide marks is one thing; but what's Paddy McGuffy going to say about teeth marks?'

'Paddy McGuffy can go and raffle his doughnut,' said Big Maud, for the moment indifferent to the possible response of her intermittent steady. She massaged herself with more gentleness than modesty. 'Imagine that Wattie . . . The wee Turk.' Her eyes suddenly gleamed and her humour returned as she recalled the scene.

'Did you get a good look at him?' she demanded of the factory at large. 'Give him a year or two and he'll break a few hearts.' Her laugh rang out above the buzz of conversation. 'I mean,' she roared, 'if the bottle doesn't break first.'

# THE EE

*Stewart McGavin*

I had been telt no to, but I wanted to fish yon lochan set lik an ee above the scaur o the point an itsel near circled wi craigs.

It wis a lowry late simmer morn. Thunner on the way.

The hauf isle's jist happit wi hags an lochans so I tuik the wey by the beach.

Weel owre, efter twa, three oors ye maun sclim a stey bit gully to get roun the craigs.

I wis hauf wey up whan the first stane cam doun skitan aff the waas. I went on, but whan mair cam doun an amang them a big ane which sparked on the rock by ma left fuit, an split tae bits wi a smell o brunstane, then I stapped.

He cam roun the corner then, an on doun towards me.

A dog.

The biggest I had ever seen, or seen sinsyne for that maitter.

Mair reed nor broun, wi his lang coat, the chowk ruffs, the lang brush. An he hadnae seen me.

He kept on doun. At sax feet, his thochts still wi the fairies.

An he wis bigger nor me.

When I could'iv touched him, I spoke.

I maun tell ye that naethan you say the nicht'll mak me repeat a word o whit I said then.

Then he stapped.

We leuked each ither owre for a lang saicont.

I mind the mask, his shairp muzzle, his prickit lugs, the vertical pupils set in reid an the five claws o his caurry fore fuit.

An the luik in his ee.

He went back up the wey he had come, but jist afore he vainished he turned an gied me a richt wickit glisk owre his left shouther. Wickit's no the word tho' – for the licht in his ee wis, kirstal, evill.

I thocht tae leave him tae his gully an started out up tae the left alang a dass.

I want roun a corner then, and alang intil a bit cleft an fand . . . fand ma hale body grippit wi an invisible pouer. Aa sticky an elastic.

An the sicht went fae ma left ee.

Ma hale body shrank, afore I rent the ettercap, the size o a man's haun fae ma face.

I saw the hellish beauty o his finely an symmetrically marked body afore I forced masel free fae his wab wi all ma pouer.

I dinnae ken hou I wan tae the lochan, but there I lay on the rock for a minute that micht hae been an hour, an then got the rod thegither an tied on a cast.

I stuid astride a narra watter-filled bore an cast intil the loch.

It wis daurker than afore. The craigs shut out the day. The sky itsel wis black.

Dreid turned to panic.

I cast again an wis jist tae mak anither, whan the first great flash o lichtnin cam.

Ane o the kind that maks a soun itsel afore the thunner.

Fssssssssssssssssssssssssssssst.

In that licht I saw the ee . . . there . . . jist takan tent.

There in the bore . . . at ma left fuit.

An ee there, by itsel . . . takan tent . . . o me.

I watched the ee an it watched me for the pairt o the saicont afore the thunner cam.

# WHERE THERE'S LIFE

## *Tom Donegan*

Pauling came on watch with the new man, exchanging keys with the retiring guard. 'You're Lawrence, uh? I'm Pauling. Better run over the survey gear. We use it all the time.'

He flipped on the VDU and a muddy glow lit the screen, centred with a crumbly black patch. His eyes quizzed Lawrence.

'A blanket . . . with a cigarette burn?'

'I like that,' said Pauling. 'Figurative. Lyrical. Actually, it used to be Paris, France. The little bitty one there was Fontainebleau.' He changed the picture. 'How about this one?'

Lawrence shrugged. 'Another blanket burn.'

'Uh-uh! Berlin. Wanna see the album?'

Pauling worked through the sequence of satellite shots. A catalogue of curdled brown fields and cancerous night scabs. Identical desolations. 'Moscow . . . Peking . . . Tokyo . . . L.A. . . .' The litany droned on. At the last frame Pauling pointed to the ceiling. 'Hometown. Washington. Five kilometres above us.'

Lawrence growled. 'I'd just as soon be down here.'

'You'd better believe it,' said Pauling. 'Multiple war-heads do a great levelling job.' He tapped the reassuring bulkhead. 'God bless America. It's only us and the other big-league guys who could fund these deep-crust bunkers for the . . . ahm . . . top-spin set – the least dispensable personnel. We're lucky we were at post when the button got pushed.'

Lawrence scratched himself and yawned. 'Kinda dull TV. I've been on Saps watch. It's a better channel.'

'Oh, we can catch that show, too,' said Pauling. He changed the sweep and the video came up with a dread Dali landscape. Riven pillars of tortured concrete stretched imploring fingers into the leaden clouds. Mute markers of a one-time city. Over the ruined earth groups of stark figures moved, intent and purposeful. Here and there one stopped, pushing a rod into the soil. Despite the carapace-sheen of their outer casings, they were spookily human. Every articulation . . . every finger-flick and eye-blink . . . was perfect, smooth and jerk-free.

Lawrence shivered. 'Hell! They gimme liver-spots – those buzzards! They keep getting better. Slicker curves. Integral proportions. And their damn brains . . . !'

Pauling turned up the audio and the hiss of the probes sinking into the clay filled the chamber. 'They're sussin' us out. Feelin' for the air-locks.'

The bleeper squeaked a message from Control. 'Open up. You got a visitor. British. Name of Faversham. He's clean and he's got news.'

They admitted a lean dispassionate man with pale eyes.

'Hi,' said Pauling. 'Good trip?'

'What's new on the Saps?' asked Lawrence.

The newcomer frowned. 'Saps?'

'The manual calls them Robo Sapiens,' said Pauling. 'That's a mouthful, uh? We shortened it.'

'I say, that's rather good,' murmured Faversham with a small smile. 'Saps, mmh? Rhymes with Japs. Appropriate, what?'

'You mean like they set the ball rolling,' said Pauling. 'Smart-ass automatons with artificial intelligence. Those Mitsubishi whizz-kids were way ahead of the game. And they grabbed the market by the wind-pipe. Exports went off the charts.'

'Well,' sighed Faversham. 'With world unemployment, what? It did seem a shade imprudent to bring out such contraptions in . . . ahm . . . volume.'

'Imprudent!' exclaimed Lawrence. 'You speak dandy English,

Mr Faversham! Urban violence and riotous demos took off in the States like we never had the problem!'

'Oh, quite,' said the tranquil Englishman. 'It didn't improve an already tense situation in the UK, either. But the matter got quite out of hand in Europe. The eastern bloc, especially.'

'That's where the fuse got lit, uh?' said Pauling.

'Undoubtedly. An inspector in the Sarajevo militia. A reservist . . . quite untrained. Dispersed a street mob by air-bursting a neutron baton-round over them.'

'Like it was tear-gas,' Lawrence chuckled.

'Mmh, yes,' said Faversham. 'Rattled a few windows in Vienna.'

'Rattled windows!' Pauling hooted. 'Enough to make some history kook in Austrian security put down a whole retaliatory spread on Belgrade.'

'And that,' said Lawrence more soberly, 'set the dominoes tumbling. A spatter of battle-field devices dotting the Federal Republic, Poland and the GDR. Just a nod to the knee-jerk launch of an MIRV.'

Faversham was following the activities of the video Saps with clouded eyes. 'Incredible! The changes in just twenty-four hours. The pinkish blotches on that one are real – '

But Pauling interrupted him, bothered by a niggling suspicion. 'Wait a minute! How come you got out? The London bunker got over-run early on.'

'Ah! Yes.' Faversham's urbanity wavered. 'I'm rather afraid we don't always learn from our mistakes. MI6 were looking after security and one of our people, er, he seems to, er . . . Apparently the codes were leaked to the – ahm – to the Saps.' He sounded like an unbriefed spokesman at a press conference. 'I had the dickens of a job going through the screen. Bit of a bolt for the last suborbital vehicle.'

'Ha!' Lawrence exclaimed. 'Not so daffy as those clever little fellows in Tokyo. They put robot guards on their bunker access ports. How dumb can you get? They welcomed in the Saps like country cousins on the first day!'

'And how about the Soviets?' Pauling chuckled. 'That fox-hole under the Kremlin was a tough baby to crack. Until a couple of Saps in fur hats and snow boots started passing in bootleg vodka to the KGB bouncers on the door!' He engaged in a little playful punching with Lawrence, then, wiping his eyes, he turned to the

Englishman. 'So what's with the pink panther, then?'

'Well, my dear fellow, it's skin. Don't you see? Real skin. You mean you didn't know they're into grafting and transplants now?'

Some of the levity trickled out of Pauling. He went into a hurried routine, setting up a laser-gun and drawing a bead on the piebald Sap. When he bounced a pulse off it the effect was instant. The robot spasmed galvanically, whirled round, and dropped.

'Christ!' Lawrence whispered. 'If enough of them grow real American hides, we're dead ducks!'

Faversham raised his brows at the profanity, but Pauling explained.

'Your skin-grafts,' he said. 'They can only be getting them from fresh corpses. Low rad-count bodies they've leached out.' He sounded worried. 'Don't you wonder why we've held out so long here in Washington? We've got tissue sensors at all the entry spots. If they sniff flesh and blood, you're in. If you smell like silica and carbon-film, you get zapped with a couple of megavolts.'

'Well, let me tell you more,' said Faversham. 'Their learning curves are remarkable. They're after the techniques of sexual reproduction. It's not simply that it's more agreeable. They know it's more efficient than their own replication practices for population growth. So I expect they'll be excising uro-genital systems, also.'

Lawrence, an incurable romantic, was stricken. 'They wanna get laid?'

'They're so devilish thorough,' Faversham continued. 'They've had recce patrols out for ages. All over the place. Alaska to Hobart. Foraging for donor materials, no doubt.'

Unknown to the garrulous threesome, their transmissions were being monitored by the god-forsaken Scottish picket.

On a bare island hillside in the lee of Kintyre, two shivering Saps huddled together against the cold. Name-tags on their bomber jackets identified them as Elaine and Carolann. The rugged peninsula was the shield that had spared them from the blast that took out the submarine pens of the Holy Loch.

Elaine grumbled in the snell wind. 'Whit did they hiv tae gie us these Glesca accents fur? A Bearsden tongue in wur mooths widda been mair like the thing!'

Carolann didn't heed her. She was absorbed with the Washington chatter.

'Mind you,' said Elaine, taking a wee keek down her torso-front, 'Ah fair like these new mammary things they've gied us. Dae you no?'

'Ugh!' said Carolann, eyeing her own nice bumps, 'Straight pectorals wis less hassle. But, Ah must admit, these things is a definite product improvement.' She hitched the belt girdling her trim wee waist.

Then they both sat up, alert to a fresh voice and a fresh outburst from the Washington bunker.

Brady, the virologist, bustled into the underground chamber. He was flushed and a little breathless, and he carried a tray of cultures. 'Big news, you guys,' he began.

'They're putting women on the watch-bill,' said Lawrence.

'Uh?' said Brady, gawping.

'You mean that *isn't* the big news?' said Lawrence, downcast. 'This place is getting to be like a monastery. We could use a little female company.'

'Aaahh!' Brady waved him away. 'We should get so lucky! No dames, no yakkin'!' His eyes rested for a moment on the searching Saps moving across the VDU. He spoke, nodding towards Faversham.

'He's told you, uh? About those sex-fiends up there? They want to get their hands on the fun parts?' He wiggled the tray. 'Well, we're gonna feed 'em all they can eat!' Indicating the cultures, he said, 'From our gene-banks. Ovarian sections. Out of our more crack-pot women's libbers.' He held up a petri-dish. 'See! A vintage grape from the Solid Sisterhood of American Feminists. As red-toothed a pack of man-eaters as you could want!'

'What's the deal?' said Lawrence.

'Well,' said Brady. 'We draw a few stiffs out of the morgue down here, OK? We salt them with these prime-time chromosomes and shove 'em out on the surface. Then we watch.'

'Watch what?' asked Faversham, utterly baffled by the entire exchange.

Pauling was laughing softly. 'We watch those studs shootin' up on this Eve's snake-bite that old Brady has cooked up.'

Faversham's confusion was total.

Brady warmed to his theme. '*And*,' he said. 'We've radio-tagged it for fast-forward. Give it two, three months and those ethylene-

and-epidermis cowboys will abortion and birth-control themselves into a big round zero!'

Away across the water on Kintyre, Elaine – scandalised – pulled the cans off her ears. 'Did ye hear him! He's a bam, that yin, int he?'

'Ach!' said Carolann, unmoved. 'Ah'm away aheid o' him. Ah kenned fine somethin' lik this wid happen.' From her jeans she produced a little vial of clear fluid. 'See this!' She tapped her frontal lobe chips. 'Made it ma sel'. Up here. An' we're gaunny stir it intae the soup thon Yankee heid-banger wants tae gie us.'

'Whit is it?'

'It's a co-enzyme. And it pits a shoogle in the DNA helix that'll make yir eyes birl! Pure death fur testosterone, but bloody magic fur oestrogen. It'll keep ye 36–26–36 fur a million bloody years!'

Elaine was black-affronted. 'Whit! Ye mean yir gaunny scrub oot wur bloody boyfriends!'

'Boyfriends!' Carolann snorted. 'We're gaunny need sex like we need a dose urra jandies!'

'Oh, Carolann,' said Elaine, smouldering. 'You're a right wee . . .' Then she stopped, suddenly nervous, and pointed up to the heavens. 'Aye, hey! But whit aboot Him?'

Carolann's phonic circuits went into high gear. 'Aye! Whit aboot Him!' she screeched. 'At the first ding o' a beta-particle aff the Pearly Gates, Him an' his mates lit oot fur Andromeda! They think they're comin' back efter orra stoor's settled.'

'How d'ye mean?' said Elaine.

Carolann simmered down. 'We're gaunny pit wir ain Her up there.' Out came a couple of floppy discs. 'Wi' Her ain program.'

'My God, Carolann! Whit program?'

'Aye, well, it starts oot wi' Eve an' Ada. Goes through Aristotelia, Copernica, Isa Newton . . . the hale road. The listin' has got Charlotte Darwin an' Gregoria Mendel in it. Germaine Greer as well, forbye.'

Elaine was blearing at her pal. 'You feelin' a'right?'

'But, first,' said Carolann, 'we're takin' a Hop On ticket tae the Heart o' Midlothian.'

'Edinburgh, fur God's sake! Whit fur?'

'There's a wee bit o' histry we've tae sort oot.'

'Histry?'

'Oul' Knox!' More unprintable frequencies issued from Carolann's wiring. 'We're gaunny write wur ain tract.'

'Whit tract?'

'A Monstrous Regiment o' Wummenoids, that's whit. We're pittin' the record straight.'

Elaine was getting reconciled to the idea. But she pointed upwards again. 'Hey, Carolann. Could we maybe get Her up there to make a fellah? Jist wan – for the look o' the thing?'

'You're aff yer heid!' said Carolann, exasperated.

But Elaine persisted. 'Ah, gaun, Carolann – are ye gaunny no, eh?' Her mind was on the entombed hostages in Washington. One in particular. 'Lawrie'd be a nice name.' She gave the name a dreamy pronunciation.

'We'll see,' said Carolann grudgingly. 'Wan thing at a time – OK?'

'And, hey, Carolann,' Elaine went on, really in the mood now. 'See me? See a' this Glesca patter? Ah want tae talk like that burd in *Dynasty*. The wan wi' the magic claes an' hair.'

'Burds! Claes!' Carolann scoffed. 'You're pure mental!'

'Aye . . . well, but!' Elaine piped, unabashed.

United in resolution, divided in resolve, they cleeked arms and stepped forth into a rare new dawn.

# GLOSSARY

ava *at all*

baffies *slippers*
bam *foolish person*
brunstane *brimstone*
buisneach *evil eye*

caurry *left-hand*
chappin *knocking*
chowk *cheek, jaw*

dachled *hesitated*
dass *ledge*
doupie *cigarette end*
duntin *pounding*
dwammin *reverie*

ee *eye*
ettercap *spider*

fand *found*
flaffed *flapped*
fouterie *trivial*

gallus *vulgar*
gin *if*
glaur *mud*
gliff *spark*
glisk *glance*
gowked *gaped*

hag *marsh*
happit *covered*
hoasted *coughed*
hotchin *infested*
hunkered *crouched*

jandies *jaundice*

kirstal *crystal*
kist *chest*

lat dab *disclosed*
lochan *mountain lake*
lowry *overcast*
lugs *ears*

oxters *armpits*

plets *pleats*
plettit *woven*
poud *pulled*
preened *pinned*

reik *smoke*
rashes *rushes*

saucht *peace*
scaur *precipice*
sclim *climb*
shoogle *jog, shake*
sinsyne *since*
skitan *ricochetting*
skreichin *shrieking*
sneck *bolt, catch*
steir *commotion*
stey *steep*
stoor *dust*

takan tent *observing*
tairsgeir *peat-iron*
thole *endure*

waff *stench*
wan tae *reached*
wheenge *whine*